Before the Clock Ticks

Stephen Santos

© 2020 by Stephen Santos

All rights reserved. No part of this publication may be reproduced, stored in a retrieval system, or transmitted in any form or by any means--for example, electronic, photocopy, recording--without the prior written permission of the author. The only exception is brief quotations in printed reviews.

All characters, names, places and incidents are fictional, and any resemblance to actual events, locales or persons, living or dead, is coincidental.

Cover Design by: Lindsey Bucher

This book is dedicated to my best friend.

You found me when I was lost
You loved me when I was wrong
And You led me on the path to freedom
Even when I was not the most enjoyable travel companion

I will forever be grateful to you,
I owe you my life!

Thank you Jesus.

Introduction

What exists before the beginning?

Before any of us wakes up? Before our eyes receive the rays of sunshine or the light from manufactured fixtures? These hit our sense of vision like cold water splashed in one's face in the early morning.   It is like the shock to your system after the plunge into icy waters. The gasp that overtakes your lungs when as if in an instant, everything is new, different and filled with feelings that are unrecognizable.

Welcome to birth…

But is this your true beginning?

__Prologue__

"This here is the makings of a good garden," Ammoris says as he walks through the gate into where I'm sitting amidst rich soil and anticipated potential.

"You know, I love just sitting here and thinking about all the space and possibilities. But I really don't know where to begin."

"My friend, don't you worry that will come."

"May I come with you? On your walk?" I say.

"I was hoping you'd ask, come on," he says with a smile.

We begin to walk along a trail that borders the most beautiful lake. We are headed to the mountain. This is the place where he has taught me so many things.

"Where is Siloh?" He asks.

"He was sitting in the field taking care of the lamb that was just born this morning," I respond.

"Oh, that's right. What a beautiful lamb she is."

"Yeah, Siloh is enamored with animals, so this is a big day for him."

"I imagine. Tell me Alois, what is it that you are enamored with?"

"I don't know Ammoris…. I really don't know. I mean, I like our walks. I love hearing stories from the other lands, and how everything is so perfectly fit like a puzzle. I guess, I just like being with you Ammoris."

"Thank you son. And I love being with you as well. Now come along let's climb this mountain. I have something special I want to show you today."

"I can't wait," I say excitedly.

As we arrive at the top of the mountain we walk up to a stack of large rocks.

"Now, Alois, what is it that I've taught you about these rocks?"

"That they are incredibly important in the other world?"

"Yes, my son, that is right. They are. And we make a stack of them like this because…?" He says motioning me to finish his sentence.

"Because the rocks are a witness and when we put them in a pile like this, the winds and rain and other terrible forces of the other world cannot destroy the witness."

"That's it, my boy. Alois, you are at the top of your class, which is why I have a very important thing to talk to you about."

At that he sat down on the soft grass beside the pile of rocks and took a small pouch out of his hand.

"Here sit down son," he says as he motions me over."

I walk to him and sit down, knowing that this is a sacred moment.

He pulls a pouch out from his cloak.

"What is it?" I ask.

"These my son are treasures of the other world. They are what you cannot understand here because there is no antitheses to them that exists here."

With that he empties the pouch into his hand and out pours jewels, beautiful stones that sparkle in the light surrounding us. There is a ruby, topaz, emerald, sapphire, amethyst, beryl, onyx, jasper, jacinth, agate, carbuncle, and diamond.

"Ammoris, they're beautiful, what are they?"

"My dear Alois, I am allowing you to see these as the other world sees them. But, now look," he says as he waves his other hand over them.

I can no longer see them with my eyes, only with my heart. And as I look closer, trying to see them with my eyes, although they stay elusive to my vision, I can feel them stronger and stronger. Feelings that existed naturally within myself, but now I am able to identify them individually. Goodness overwhelms me as I smile, and look at Ammoris. Joy, yes, joy it feels like the solidity of a large rock and the lightness of a cloud. Shalom feels like a river with its gentle waves washing over me. As I feel this thing called hope, I now know that anything is possible, that if I had ever known what chains were, they would now be falling off of me. A confidence wells up around me causing me to look directly in Ammoris's eyes. He smiles as he recognizes the look of faith that is flowing through my being.

He shuffles his hand and I know that the one rock that was holding up all the others is now on top, and a force hits me like I dare not try to describe in words. I fall backward unable to move and just allow this essence to surround me, embrace me, and overwhelm me.

He reaches over and touches my arm. "That my son, is love."

"How do you describe this love, Ammoris," I mumble through shaking lips.

"You don't son, you only receive it and know when it is present."

He takes the stones and places them back in the leather pouch and tucks them into his cloak. After I regain the ability to move again, I sit up and look at him with wide eyes.

"Now, understand Alois, you were only able to feel these treasures because for this moment I took away your present state of consciousness. In other words, I allowed you to feel what it would be like to exist in the other world and come in contact with them."

"Wow, thank you. Which one is your favorite?"

"Ha, well I have many favorites, but my prized one is the diamond," he said.

"I can see why," I smile.

"Yes, I know you can. It is the only one that those down there can offer back to me."

"And how do they do that?"

"It is through obedience, and it unlocks a treasure for me and for them. They cannot truly experience the others without first finding this one."

"Is it difficult to find?"

"Yes, very, for it takes dying to find it."

"I don't understand? How could they die down there and still find it?"

"It is ok, there are things that are very difficult to see from this side, as it is difficult to see from the other side to up here."

"How incredible it must be to live there."

"My son, it is filled with both amazement and agony. It is far different from being here. There is so much I've told you, but so much more to know. However, it wouldn't help anyone who is going there."

"Why not?"

"Well, you see the passage to the other world cannot be taken with memories. It must be this way."

"That's so sad. Why must it be this way?"

He turns to me with a look of sadness but confidence in his eyes.

"Because at the heart of every journey is a place called home. It is the place that all must leave, and the place that all are searching for. There is a resistance to regaining what is lost on the journey… Alois?" He says as he looks deeply and seriously into my eyes. "You must leave me for a lifetime, but I am confident you will return for eternity."

"Ammoris I don't understand? I don't want to leave. I love being here."

"I know son, and I love having you with me, but it is necessary. The other world needs you and you need this."

"How long is a lifetime?"

"Time does not begin or end here, so you would not be able to understand it. However, even if you could understand it, you wouldn't remember it when you arrived," he says as he smiles sincerely.

He pauses and places his hand against his chest where he placed the pouch of stones.

"These exist in that world, but you will need to search to find them, and do not be deceived by your eyes. This, however," he says as he pulls a small circular device from his pocket, "is a very handy tool. It will not work until you find the one that can make the needle inside of it move. But, it will be helpful on your journey."

With that he places the device inside of my chest, smiles and places his hand over my eyes.

In an instant I am asleep floating along as if I was in a cloud. I naturally turn over to my side and curl up.

As I ponder everything we had just talked about, the memory of it all begins to fade. I become increasingly aware of a distant drumming. The consistent beat of warmth and care. I feel a presence surrounding me, like that of the one I had left, but can no longer remember his name or what he looked like. I feel this presence move over my body as if it is shaping me, forming me, but into what?

And it is here that I am learning to wait, I can not do much else. Since the moment I entered this place that beating has been marking my existence, it is a constant reminder that I'm not alone here, even though I can't see anything, and I'm not sure who or what or where I am. It is speaking to me telling me that things inside of me and all around me are all moving forward.

Chapter 1

268 days later...

All of the sensations I feel here are safe and comfortable. The squeeze is the only one I don't understand. I'm not exactly sure what it is about. It happens from time to time and lately, it's been getting stronger. I've had a lot of time to ponder. I don't have much to ponder, I mean, I can't see anything, I have a very distant sense of a memory of my existence before this and I have no clue what is ahead, but I am able to feel sensations like never before. Just the other day, someone who felt like they were somehow a part of me, began speaking to me, and then pressed their lips against wherever I am right now. I felt warmth, and protection and love when this happened. Love, I have a feeling about this. Like I experienced it before. If feels like knowing I'm supposed to be right here.

I decide to do some stretches. First I push one part down and then the next, then I decide to push these things up here out, and ahhh, that feels good, now, all at once and go, go, go, go. I stop as I hear moaning coming from somewhere beyond me. I hope I didn't cause that. Oh well, back to stretching.

I start to feel some squeezing. There is a commotion like none I've experienced. I've heard sounds before, some that I honestly think were directed toward me, but this is different. I smile as I am sloshed around.

All of a sudden a squeeze comes, stronger than any of the others. That didn't feel good at all. That squeeze started to push me out of my home. I'm trying to struggle as the next one comes but I don't have a lot of strength in my arms and legs, even with all the workouts I've been doing.

My living quarters have suddenly become very small. It appears as if I'm being moved somewhere, but I don't have any say where I'm going. Apparently I'm just along for the ride.

As the light becomes brighter, for the first time I'm touched by something. It is gentle and feels safe. As the pressure releases from all around me, I am immediately cold. The sensation of brightness to my eyes is overwhelming. The loudness surrounding me causes me to cry out, and it feels as if every nerve in my body is firing at the same time. So many sensations at once. I cry as air goes into my lungs for the first time. And in the midst of all of this happening at once, I hear it.

The tick of the clock.

Immediately I am placed against warmth. I feel a touch on my back, and then another. The feeling of safety wrapped around me, calms all of the chaos. And in this safe place I hear the familiar drum sound that has filled my existence. The consistency and warmth, the reminder that I wasn't alone here. It is you, I think as I look up into the most beautiful eyes. She whispers and smiles and it warms me up inside and out. I'm then met with another sensation. A kiss from another that I know is a part of me. He whispers something I cannot understand yet, but I know that it is filled with this love that I experienced before. I think this will probably be the best place ever, if only I can stay right here.

Chapter 2

3 years later…

It has been a whole lot of time that has passed. I still have that distant memory that sometimes passes through my mind. It's like it's on the tip of my brain, but I just can't grasp it. It feels like a land that I want to go hide away in. Especially when things are tough here at home. I still feel those feelings of warmth and love when my dad kisses me on the forehead. And when my mom wraps me up in her arms I know I can heal from any hurt and overcome any difficulty, but sometimes the difficulties aren't my own, they are just something I have to bear. I guess mom and dad are upset about something because I've seen them with angry eyes a lot more lately. I wish there was something I could do to stop it.

Normally, Samantha, my sister, just takes me by the hand and brings me up to her room. We play with her toys, or she reads me a book and tells me everything will be ok. Lately, when it's gotten worse, I've been scared. I'm not sure what of, just this feeling that everything might not be ok.

Other than those times, my life is really fun. Everybody seems to think I'm cute and I honestly like it when they look at me and cheer me on. I'm learning some really difficult things. Like just the other day I jumped off the last step of the stairs. It must have been like 10 feet tall. I did it like a champ with a little wobble at the end. And with all the cheering and claps and everybody watching me, what else was I to do but do it again, and again. I mean, as long as they are looking for a show, I'm gonna give them one. After about the 17th time I decided I needed to take a break.

The other day I had another new experience, but it wasn't a good one. I did something they told me was bad. I didn't know that the special markers weren't made for dad's work bag. I thought this would be the best picture for him to take to work every day and remember me by. But apparently, I was wrong. And there I was in my room. I sat there on my bed with my hands on my lap and the biggest pouty face I could muster. It was at that moment that I felt this new feeling. I was sorry for what I did. Even though dad had always told me that we only draw on paper and not on walls or furniture or other things. His work bag just looked like the perfect canvas and I was feeling like this picture would be the one I became famous for. This feeling that seemed like a thick coat that was wrapped around my shoulders felt as strong as when I jumped off the stair but instead of wanting people to look at me, I just wanted to hide. I was mad at myself, mad at the markers, and mad at anything else I could think of. Mom told me later that the feeling I had was called shame and that I would feel this many times over the course of my life, but that I shouldn't let it hold me down. Then she told me about forgiveness and that it was like a cleaning sponge that could clean anything. I asked if it could clean off dad's work bag. She just laughed and said, 'I don't think so dear.'

Chapter 3

12 years later...

I can't help but be utterly frustrated with my parents. I mean seriously, they have life so easy. They get lots of money for working and they get to eat what they want. They call all the shots, and what's better in life than that.

For instance, sleeping in would be nice now and again. School can't be that important that I have to be there every single day. But, with my parents, if the doors are open then we are there. It's the same with church. I'll be honest, all the talk about living a good life, but no real reasons for why. At least I have some friends there. That at least keeps me sane.

It's funny I still feel like a little kid half the time, trapped by my parent's decisions. They say where to go, and I just have to follow. But, not for long. Next year, I get my driver's license, and I can already taste the freedom. Me and my friend Andy took my sister's car out for a spin the other day. We hit 35 mph in the neighborhood. Man, that felt so good, I just can't wait to get my license.

Other than that, life is pretty even. I go to school, I go to soccer practice, I like girls and some of them like me. I try to be a nice guy because it seems like that gets me further, but really I'm just trying to get through this stage of life more than anything.

So, the other night I had this crazy dream. Some guy that I've never seen before, handed me all these jewels. He put them right in my hand, and I remember thinking, 'I am gonna be rich'. He looked at me and said, "Don't be deceived." When I looked down they were gone, and I remember trying to look really hard at my hand, but I couldn't see anything. He said to me, "What do you feel?"

I said, "I don't feel anything."

I looked up at him and a tear fell down his cheek.

"I know you don't," he said. "Find home, don't forget the compass I gave you."

I woke up and was super bummed, because I had probably 80k worth of jewels in my hand and now nothing. I mean I could've bought a ride that would've made even the really rich kids jealous.

What does that even mean? Don't be deceived. Deceived by what? And why do I need to find a home? I already have a house. And what compass?

Needless to say, I was thoroughly confused and chalked that one up to late-night pizza, the night before.

Other than that dream, nothing much has been happening here. I still think about it from time to time and wonder what it meant.

My dad keeps me busy helping him with his business in the summers. It's not really my cup of tea. It's actually really hard work. I end up carrying a lot of stuff for him and bringing him tools and sometimes he lets me sand the wood that he's working on. But at least I'm making some money.

"Lewis, can you grab me my chisels?"

"Sure dad, here you go."

"Thanks son," he says as he stops what he is doing and looks over at me.

"Are you doing ok?"

"Yeah, I'm fine. Just working for the weekend," I say smiling.

"Yeah, I've been there. You know Lewis, work is not a curse, how it feels sometimes, and our wrong perspectives about it, are the curse. But work, for us men, it is a part of our DNA. It's how God made us."

"I don't know Dad, this doesn't seem very fun or fulfilling to me. This is more your thing than mine."

"I know, I know, but no matter what you find yourself doing for work, your perspective about it will either make it something that takes from you, or that fills you up. I honestly believe that you can have the worst job ever and still gain something from it."

"Yep, it's called a paycheck dad," I say with the sarcasm that a fifteen-year-old boy can get away with.

"See, there's my point."

"What point?"

"You have the wrong perspective about work. Someday it will change through the process of life, but even if I told you now how to fix it. You wouldn't be able to."

"Yeah, I could."

"Haha, I love your enthusiasm and confidence son, but the ticking of the clock is what allows us to grow and change. We may be able to see the truth about something but to live in it, for it to become a part of who we are, takes a process that takes time. For some people, it takes more time than for others. Like you, for instance, it might take you a little while," he says as he laughs, pulls me over to hug me and kisses me on the forehead.

I push him away and straighten my shirt, "Thanks Dad."

As much as I don't want affection from my dad right now, I feel safe here, provided for, and loved.

Chapter 4

7 years later…

I think I'm in love. Her name is Sara and she is… amazing. I saw her last week from across the cafeteria. When she looked over toward me she smiled, and that smile lit up every single lightbulb in my body. I know that love isn't something you rush into, and that this isn't some high school relationship. This is college, way different. I think I'm going to ask her out today. I've seen her walking from her dorm room to class a few times, and she just seems so different from the other girls.

I've been standing here for over an hour and no sign of her. As I decide to walk back to my dorm I hear 2 girls laughing as they are heading toward me. There she is.

I smile as I approach them.

"Hi, uh Sara? Right?"

"Yeah. Do I know you?"

"Um, yeah, we saw each other in the cafeteria, I mean I guess I thought you saw me or, well I just wanted to say hi," I say rather awkwardly.

"Oh, hi," she smiles with that smile again.

"Well, I'll see you around," she says as she continues to walk by, giggling with her friend.

6 months later…

I finally popped the question. I mean I was ready to ask her to marry me the day we met, but between the advice my dad gave me and me actually listening this time, I think we came up with a better plan.

If all goes according to schedule we will be happily married in about 5 months, which is right after graduation. By then I'll have landed my dream job and be able to get us into an apartment, just for a very short time of course. That will buy us some time while we are looking for a house that fits us, and by fits us, I mean, is awesome.

I can't believe it, life is finally what I've dreamed of. It's like the world has opened up before me and I just can't wait to get going.

A couple months ago I took Sara back to my parent's house to meet the family. Everything went great, and everyone loved her. We even went to church with my family. It's not that I stopped believing in God, I just haven't had as much of a need I guess. And there aren't really any churches around our campus, at least not ones that I've tried.

The strangest thing happened at church. So the pastor started talking about joy, and peace, and hope, and love, and immediately my mind was taken back to the dream I had when I was 15. The one where the guy who was like my dad was giving me the jewels that were in his hand. Somehow there was a correlation between those jewels and the things the pastor was talking about. It felt like I somehow understood this, or at least knew about it, but I really don't have a clue what it means.

And then he went on to talk about a compass that God placed inside of our chest to lead us home. As soon as he said that, I felt my whole body jerk as I gasped. It felt like something was lodged inside of my chest. Everyone turned to look at me. My mom leaned over and asked if I was ok. I just shrugged and said, "I don't know what that was."

After church everyone seemed really concerned.

"Did it feel like your heart? You know Grandpa had a heart attack when he was younger," my dad said.

"Oh John, stop that, Lewis is not having a heart attack," Mom replied.

Sara snuggled up next to me on the couch. "Are you ok?" She said with concern in her voice.

"Yeah, I'm uh, not sure what that was, but I'm fine now."

"I'll tell you what it was," said Samantha, my sister. "That there was the Holy Spirit. I've heard about this, people start bouncing around and they can't control themselves at all. You better watch out little brother, soon you'll be flopping down the aisle like a fish."

"Oh Samantha, stop that," Mom said as everyone else chuckled.

"C'mon Mom, after all the years of him teasing me relentlessly," she said with a smile.

"Guys it's actually somehow connected to this dream I had when I was 15. I never told anyone about it. But it came back to me this morning and I think it has something to do with what happened this morning."

"Honey, will you tell us about it?" Said Mom.

"Yeah, sure." I went on to tell them about the dream, but nobody had much to say about it. They all just looked at me, and then nodded and went on their way.

Somehow this held much more weight for me than it did for them. I spent the rest of that week reaching up to feel my chest, wondering what caused me to jump like that, and why after 7 years, that dream was coming back to me. I'll be honest, all of this feels strangely familiar but I have no recollection of anything that would make it familiar.

Chapter 5

2 years later…

Let's just say that life has not been what I pictured. I've been stuck at a customer service desk at a local retail store, Sara is pregnant, our apartment that was supposed to be short-term doesn't look like it has an end in sight and I don't feel like I have any value on this earth.

Sara seems to not be phased by the way things are like I am, but I also don't think she's carrying the weight of this like I am. We've been going to a church down the road from our apartment and it seems like she likes it there. I don't really see the point in it. It doesn't seem like it's changing anything for us. I mean, I talk to God. I ask Him what in the world He's doing. I ask Him for a little help here and there. I guess I'm just feeling overwhelmed with this whole baby thing and feeling like we are not going anywhere. Sometimes I just wish life was easier.

I can't remember not going to church, except for maybe during college. But what did it ever change? I mean the only thing I can see is that I would feel a little bit better after leaving, but by the end of Monday, I would feel the same as before. And who knows, maybe I only felt better because everybody was looking at me being there and saying good job, you made it. Just like when I was a little boy jumping off the last step. As long as people are watching and happy with me, it fills me up just enough to do it again. Maybe that's all it really is. Who knows?

I will say this though, the guys that I meet on Thursdays to play poker with, seem to have it figured out. They are all talking about their career path and how they are strategically placing themselves in positions and around certain people to ensure they get where they want to go. I just smile and nod at them.

Last week Eddie stopped in the middle of our game, looked over at me and said, "Lewis, what are you gonna do with your life?"

"What's that supposed to mean?" I replied.

"Well, I just never hear you talk about your plans or where you want to be or anything like that. Don't you want to retire early, and travel or do something that adds value to your life?"

"Of course I do, I just don't have it figured out like you guys do. It doesn't seem that easy for me."

"Dude, no one said it's easy. I worked in my dad's butcher shop for years through high school and college, and then I vowed to not end up in that line of work. So, I started talking to businessmen that I knew. I started asking for their advice and then asking for their help, and just took a lot of notes. You know? And before I knew it, one of them was asking me to come work for them doing odds and ends and then after I proved myself, I just kept climbing the ladder. It's not easy, it's just the path you choose. It's your life man, at some point, you gotta take control of it and do something."

"Yeah, I guess so. But, I don't even know why I'm here. I mean, is this really it? To just get a good job and retire early and then go on trips? It just seems so… non-climactic."

"Non-climactic? Haha, Lewis, you're funny, man. Listen, it's what our father's did, what our grandfathers did, it's what our great grandfathers did. They fought against the system in order to get on top. And now it's our journey to take. Lewis seriously, as a friend you gotta figure this out. You're gonna be a dad soon. Do you really want your kid telling his friends, that his dad still works at a mall clothing store?"

"Well, you find me a job in something better and I'll take it, deal?"

"Deal," he said smiling.

2 weeks later…

"Lewis," Eddie said on the other side of the phone.

"Yeah, hey man, how's it going?"

"Good, really good. Hey, I need you to stop by my office and fill out an application."

"For what?"

"For a job silly. Remember, we had a deal."

"Oh my goodness. Seriously? What even is the job?"

"It's entry-level customer service, but I'm sure it pays better than your current setup, and this company is growing so the chance to move up is always a possibility."

"Man are you sure you think I'm a fit for this?"

"Dude, you need help, I think at this point you just need to start trying some things," he says laughing.

"Alright, alright. When should I come by?"

"How about tomorrow morning?"

"Sounds good, thanks man."

"You got it, oh and Lewis. Wear something nice."

"Ok, like my sweatpants without the holes."

"Yeah, like those," he says laughing.

Chapter 6

2 weeks later…

I feel that thing rising up again in me. Like when I was in college. It's like all the possibilities are endless and at my fingertips. I start work at Eddie's office tomorrow. I'm supposed to wear a tie. I don't even know if I remember how to tie one. I should call my dad. He'd know.

"Oh, hi Mom, I was just trying to get a hold of dad. I start my new job tomorrow and wanted to ask him how to tie a tie."

"Oh hi honey, I'm so sorry, your father's been in bed all day. I think he just has the flu, but he's looking like he's feeling pretty rough."

"Oh I'm so sorry to hear that. Well, tell him that I said to get better, and let me know if I can bring anything over."

"Ok I will dear."

Later that week…

My new job is great. I feel awesome every time I walk through the doors. They have free coffee, snacks, a game room, and everybody seems so chill.

"Hey man," Eddie says as he walks by my cubicle.

"Hey Eddie, how's it going?"

"Good, you want to get lunch today?"

"Yeah definitely."

"Cool, I'll swing by in about an hour."

"Sounds great."

90 minutes later…

"So, what do you think of the job so far?"

"Man, this is awesome, it just feels like the place I've always wanted to be."

"That's great Lewis, I'm really glad I could help you out."

"Me too, thank you."

"Listen, just to give you a heads up. The guys who run this company are innovators and they are looking for people who are constantly willing to go the extra mile and spin new ideas. So, just make sure you're bringing your A-game, and those promotions will be rolling in."

"Got it. Will do."

Just then my phone rings. It's my mom.

"Hey, I'm gonna take this real quick," I say as I stand up from the table.

"Yeah, no problem," he responds.

"Hi Mom, how's it going?"

"Not good honey," she says through crying.

"Mom, what's wrong?"

"Your dad, he is in the hospital, and it's not good."

"What is it?"

"It's an infection that we didn't catch and it's through his blood. It's not good, Lewis, you should come right away."

"Ok, Mom, I'll be right there," I say as I hang up the phone.

"Eddie, I gotta go man. My dad is in the hospital, and it's not looking good."

"Oh man, I'm so sorry. Yeah, go. I'll let your manager know what happened. Keep me updated and let me know if there's anything I can do to help."

"Ok, thanks man, I will."

5 months later…

Life goes up and down from the crest of one wave to the trough before the next. And we never know how low the trough or how high the crest. It seems we are only along for the ride. I finally had something to hope in. This new beginning, this job that was filling me up, and now it all feels so grey, so lifeless.

I'm still punching in and punching out, but the drive to do anything more is non-existent.

Sara's belly is getting big and in the wake of all the sadness from losing dad, there's a lot of talk and excitement about this new addition to our family.

Thanks to this new job it looks like we'll be able to buy a house in the next 6 months, which should allow us just enough time to settle before our baby arrives.

I still can't believe he's gone. Less than a year ago we went fishing out on the lake. He was telling me about how proud he was of me. I laughed when he said it.

"Seriously Dad, I'm not really doing much that would make you proud."

"Son when you're a father, you'll understand what it is that makes us proud."

"Alright Dad," I say chuckling.

"Lewis, can I tell you something that I've never told anyone before."

"Sure Dad."

"When you were born. The moment you came out, I had this crazy feeling that you were something special."

"Thanks Dad."

"No, you're not hearing me. It's like there was a really special purpose that was placed on your life. I never found out what that meant, I just remember that feeling was real strong."

"Well, I guess we'll find out, hopefully."

"Yes, you will Son. I am confident of that."

"Dad, do you ever wish you did something else in life?"

"Other than being a carpenter?"

"Yeah, like did you ever want to be a businessman?"

"You know Son, some people fall into their path, and other's trade their path for one they think looks better or feels better. But I realized after years of swinging a hammer, that no matter what path I was on, I would never be satisfied without God. I learned to love what I was doing, no matter what I was doing, because I found a friend who was right beside me through it all."

"Mom?"

"No, not your mother, although she has been with me through it all. Lewis, I know we made you go to church all growing up. We were hoping that it would be some connection for you with Jesus, not just a religion that you felt guilted into. But that journey is only yours to take Son. Jesus is the friend I'm talking about. It's taken me years to finally understand it and live in it, but now that I do. I feel like I've accomplished all that I need to on this earth."

"Huh, well I'll have to think about that."

"Yeah, just don't spend too much time trying to think about it with your head. It's more of a heart journey."

"I don't really understand, Dad."

"Don't worry Son, you will."

My memory is interrupted as Eddie peaks his head into my cubicle.

"Hey man, how are you doing?" Eddie says.

"Oh, good. I was just…"

"Man, it's ok. I can't imagine losing my dad."

"Ok, thanks."

"You coming to play poker tonight?"

"Yeah, I'll be there."

"Awesome, I'll see you there."

Chapter 7

Years later...

"Hey babe," Sara says with a sleepy smile as I walk back into the room from my morning coffee time.

"Hi honey," I respond.

"You headed to work?"

"Yeah, in a little bit."

"Lewis?" she says with hesitance.

"Yeah, honey."

"Is it any better this morning?"

"Yeah, I think so, I'm not sure, but probably."

"Oh good, I was praying for you last night and hoping it would be."

"Thanks, honey," I say not wanting to lead on that nothing has changed.

As I look in the mirror and begin to shave I recognize that something is not in the face that stares back at me. I look deep trying to figure out what's missing. What is it?

Ah yes, it's confidence. There is no confidence in that man staring back at me, which is very telling of what is in the depths of my soul.

God, why? I breathe out of my lungs in a whisper. I've done all that I can, haven't I?

"Lewis, don't forget Sammy's soccer game is tonight at 5 at the school," Sara hollers from the room.

"Ok honey, I won't."

As I turn back to the mirror a thought passes through my mind. 'Why stay where you are?'

I begin to ponder this question and then in an instant, another thought passes through like a phantom. 'Why not leave, for good?'

"But where would I go," I mumble.

"What's that babe," Sara asked through the door of the bathroom.

"Oh nothing… just thinking about whether or not to keep the mustache."

"Kill it babe, trust me on this one," she says laughing.

"Nice," I reply.

The two things I can always count on Sara for is her opinion and a laugh. I kind of like the mustache. Besides, I know a lot of people have been trying to bring it back for a couple of years, but I think it's finally gaining some traction. It reminds me of my dad growing up. He always had a mustache. I guess it's one of those comfort things. Plus, my mom always says, 'If you got it, flaunt it.' Not sure that's the best advice, but in this situation, I think it might work.

Well, time to get to my job that pays our bills, at least most of the time.

"Bye honey," I say as I walk out the door trying to hide my mustache that I've managed to save for at least one more day.

"You stinker," she says as she sees me covering my mouth. She runs over and puts her arms around me and reminds me that she loves me once again.

Even with all of the difficulties that come in relationships, having someone beside you through it all is what makes it worth it. My mind jumps back to those thoughts that went through my head in the bathroom. Was that me? Am I supposed to do something about all that? Are we supposed to move? Am I supposed to jump off a bridge? I laugh as I think about the silly thoughts that sometimes go through my mind.

At work, I find myself once again, unfulfilled and unsatisfied. I've been working at this job for about five years now. I can't say it's a bad job. But it's just not what I want to be doing. I'm not exactly sure what it is that I want to be doing. Maybe retirement. Yeah, that would be nice. I could be professionally retired. Meet up with some buddies every morning, have a cup of coffee and talk about sports, or stocks, or fishing. That seems like the only thing I would really like to do. Listen to me, I sound like Eddie, back when we were just out of college. That guy has really climbed the ladder and although he could retire, he seems stuck in the cycle of needing more.

"Hey Lewis," my boss says as he peeks his head in my office.

"Yeah James."

"The numbers are in from last quarter. It's not that you aren't doing a good job. You really are doing well, I just need a little more performance out of you. You know, if you could make about ten percent more calls in a day than you currently are, I think your numbers would be up to where we need them to be. Do you think you could do that for me?"

"Yeah James, I'll do my best."

"That's the spirit. You know Lewis, we are headed towards some big things with this company and you are a part of that. We need what you have to offer."

"Alright boss, I'll get right on it," I said. But what I really wanted to say was, 'your paycheck really needs what I have to offer, not the company.'

Is it ok for me to feel like I'm the one bringing in the money and yet what I get out of it is so minimal. I may not be the best salesperson here, but it's all the same in the end. I would have to work like sixty hours per week to make the numbers that James is talking about. And I'm just not willing to do that. I definitely don't want work to be my life. I actually like being home with my family. My wife is so wonderful, and Lily and Sammy… Oh no, Sammy's game. What time is it? 5:02 reads the time on my computer. I grab my coat and hurry out of the office. At least I won't be too late.

Chapter 8

I make it to the soccer field at 5:20 and snuggle up next to Sara on the bleachers on this cool October evening. She hands me her mug filled with a mix of hot chocolate and coffee.

"Mmm, a poor boy's mocha. I love it," I say smiling.

"Hey there Lily, how was your day?" I say leaning forward to see my little princess.

"Good daddy, we got to dissect a frog in science class. Most of the girls were grossed out, but I dug right in."

"That's my girl," I say as I chuckle.

She's always been the one that doesn't mind getting dirty. Even more so than her brother. Whenever she gets the chance, she's knee-deep in a creek before I have the chance to stop her. She's my tough girl. Even her big brother knows not to mess with her.

I can't believe Sammy is already 11. This whole soccer thing has really taken off for him. His coaches think he's a natural and last year he was invited to play on this club soccer team.

"Go Sammy!" we all stand up and yell in unison as he breaks away from the defense with the ball. Just him and the goalie now. Yes!!! another goal. We all stand and cheer. I get so excited when my kids excel at something. It gives me hope that there's a possibility of a better life out there for them than I've been able to have. I don't know that he'll become a professional soccer player, but maybe it will get him into college. Lord knows my job won't pay his way.

"Hey Babe?" Sara says as she leans over into me. "Are you okay with pizza for dinner? I didn't have a chance to make anything.

"You know me. Food is fuel, and if it tastes good too, then that's just a bonus," I say wondering if anybody else cares as little about what they're eating as I do. I guess I just don't see the point in having everything fancy. Just give my body what it needs to keep going and I'm good.

After another victory for Sammy's team we head out to celebrate at the local pizza joint.

We arrive home and the kids head upstairs to bed. I plop on the couch and turn on the television as Sara walks into the family room.

"Hey babe, I'm going to go to the bedroom to read for a little bit," she says as she walks over and kisses me.

"Ok, I'm just gonna watch a show then head to bed."

"Sounds good. Lewis?"

"Yeah."

"Are you doing okay?"

"Yeah, I'm fine, just need to relax in front of some melodramatic comedy," I say with a smile.

"Alright babe, love you," she says waiting for a response.

I turn to her knowing that if I don't respond with an appropriate response it will just prolong my opportunity to be entertained.

"Love you too," I reply.

I really do love my wife. She's my rock. But, sometimes I need some time alone. It's not about her, I think it's more about how us guys work.

Although it is interesting that she's been prying so much lately about how I'm doing. I think I'm fine but she seems to see something in me that I'm unaware of. Oh well, back to my show.

It's funny that so many people talk like they own t.v. shows. We all walk around the office talking about our show that was on last night. And all the funny parts, and how we weren't expecting this to happen, and how we knew that was coming. It's humorous really. Sometimes I think the show owns us more than we own the show.

Bummer, a rerun. This is a little disappointing. As I flip through the channels I find nothing that seems worthy of watching.

Your show really comes down to your personality. Some people like the stupidest shows but it's because there's a part of it that connects to their childhood memories or a dream that they have in life. It's really not up for judgment. We have many reasons as to why we watch what we watch. But the reality of all of our reasons is that we are looking for something. We spend hours each day staring at screens with millions of dots of color placed in patterns representing different stories and different lives, and all we want is to find an answer; something helpful in our lives. Sometimes the best answer is to shut up all the voices around us that are speaking of our inabilities. In reality, our failures can be the loudest voice we hear. But in t.v. land, all of that gets silenced and our brains are led on a journey that is not our own.

It's like a kid playing house. You get all the benefits without all the crappy difficulties. Well, it seems like tonight is not the night to live in t.v. land.

As I stand up I look out the back window to see my camping chair out in the middle of the backyard. My kids are always leaving my stuff out. I put on my slippers and a sweatshirt and head out back to clean up their mess. As I reach the chair something inside of myself tells me to sit down. Yeah right! I think. It's cold and there's nothing out here. Why would I just sit here? I pack up the chair and carry it back to the house.

As I crawl into bed I prepare myself for tomorrow, another day of what I already know is going to happen. Life is predictable, but how we are going to pay our bills is not always that predictable. Sara rolls over and puts her hand on my chest.

"You sure you're doing ok babe?" She says in a sleepy tone.

"Sara, I just don't know how we're gonna make it this month. Again! Why is it that we never seem to have enough?" This isn't a breakdown, it's just venting. And usually the last week of the month I need to vent.

"Babe, we're still here aren't we?"

This is her usual response. But it never helped before and it isn't helping now.

"Why does it have to be like this. I'm on this carousel of days 23 through 30 being consumed with anxiety and fear about if our power is going to be shut off and then when we barely make it by the skin of our teeth and I end up having to spend day 1 through 15 recovering. That leaves me about 8 days, 8 days a month to enjoy life. That's less than thirty percent of my life that I enjoy. That's bad, Sara. That's really bad."

"Hey, I'm right here," she says as she snuggles up close to me. "I'm not sure that's the way to look at it. We have so much to be thankful for."

"I know that, but I'm struggling to connect with any of that enjoyment."

"Do you remember what Pastor Tom spoke about on Sunday, about being thankful for what you do have? Maybe that's a part of it."

"Yeah, maybe. Sara? Can I be really honest with you?"

"Sure babe."

"I honestly don't even know if I believe any of that stuff."

"What stuff?" she said with hesitance in her voice as she sat up now fully awake.

Sara and I had grown up in church. We knew all the answers. We did all the right church stuff, and we knew all the right things to say. People looked up to us as leaders in the church. We may not have been perfect in our lives, but we were the poster children for church-goers. And here I am about to let out some very gross details about my faith.

"All of it." There I said it. "I'm afraid my faith isn't strong enough to hold up all that I've been through over the years. I'm worn out from not having answers for what we've been through and the struggle that life continues to be. I'm sorry, but I can't help what's going on."

"Ok, well do you think you just need some time off work? Or a vacation? Or maybe, I know there's this book that Julie just told me about that talks all about getting to know God better. I could ask her if we could borrow it."

"Honey, you keep asking me if I'm okay, and this is me telling you. I'm not okay! I don't know what's going on. I'm just tired of all of this."

"I'll be honest, you're scaring me a little bit, Lewis."

"I'm sorry, I don't mean to scare you, but I don't think I can un-choose what's going on inside of me. And by the way, we really have to slow down our spending with the end of the month coming."

"Sure babe, I can do that. Just wait Lewis, you'll see. God will provide this month for us again. I just know it."

"Goodnight, Honey."

"Goodnight, Babe."

We both turn to face opposite sides and I can hear her starting to cry.

Chapter 9

I spend most of the day trying to avoid my boss. It's not that I don't like my job. It just doesn't feel like a very good fit for me anymore. Sara and I both thought it was a blessing when I started there. It worked for us then, but with having kids and a mortgage it just doesn't seem to be covering us like it used to.

Sara went back to work a couple of years ago when things started getting tight. She always wanted to get back into working with kids, and although she doesn't get paid much, she loves going to work, and it definitely helps pay for some of our expenses.

So here I am sitting just offices away from some of the top salesmen in our region and I feel like the second-string guy who can't seem to make his quota no matter what the incentive is. It's not like I'm not working hard. I just don't think I'm much of a salesman.

As I walk in the house my kids greet me with hugs and kisses. It seems that no matter how bad life gets, I can just look into their eyes and all the other junk disappears, at least for that moment.

After the kids are in bed I sit down on the couch and reach for the remote. Before I can press down the 'ON' button, my gaze is redirected to the bookshelf below the t.v. One book catches my eye. It's a book my father gave me just before he passed. It's called "The art of woodworking". I lay down the remote, walk over to the bookshelf and pull out the book. As I open it, I see a note written on the inside cover from my dad. It's been 11 years since he died, and I've never really had the time or understanding to process his death. It's one of those things in life that I'm not sure you can get over. At least I couldn't. I begin to read this note for the first time. When he gave me the book, I said thanks and put it directly in the bookshelf. I never realized he had written anything in it. I probably would have read it, if I had known about this before.

I begin to read:

Lewis,
You are such a wonderful son. I'm not sure where to begin with all of what I want to say to you. But I'm sure in your life you will face..."

I snap back into reality as I hear the sound of the book hitting the hardwood floor.

"Babe, are you okay?" Sara hollers from the kitchen.

"Uh, yeah. Yeah, I'm fine, just dropped something."

I quickly take account of myself. There are tears rolling down my cheeks and my hands feel incredibly shaky. I look out back at the old garage and decide to take a walk. I grab the book and walk outside. As I slide open the heavy barn style door to this old wooden garage. I see the tools that used to be my dad's. It's funny, I knew he loved to work with his hands, but I never understood why he would choose that over a desk job. All of my friends and I agreed that we would work in an office and that's where the real money was made.

As I reach for the light switch I'm amazed at how much stuff he had. After he passed, my mom told me that he wanted me to have all of his woodworking tools. Since I didn't have any use for them, I put them back here. It seemed like a proper place to keep this stuff. As I walk past saws, and sanders and drills I place my hand on each one. Something in me stirs. I look down at the book in my hand and decide to read the rest of the note from my dad. I brush off an old office chair that's in the corner and sit down.

Lewis,

You are such a wonderful son. I'm not sure where to begin with all of what I want to say to you. But I'm sure in your life you will face things that don't make sense, things that cause wounds and pain and confusion beyond the capacity of your mind. I've seen it, Lewis. I've seen men and women break in half because of all that life can bring to their table. Lewis, there may be a day when your life feels like it's breaking in half. Sometimes, things need to break to get to what's inside. Don't be afraid when this happens. Just keep going. Every day has purpose, whether you see it or not.

I didn't buy this book for you because I wanted you to be just like me. I bought it for you because of what working with my hands has done for me. You see, it wasn't too long ago that I found myself broken in half. I know you didn't know much about this. You were young. I sat you down and told you that I needed to go away for about a month. It ended up being three. I know you didn't understand what was going on then. I'm not sure that I completely comprehend it. All I know is that those three months, saved my life. When we have a perspective of life that things don't seem to be fitting into, the only good option is to search for a new perspective.

I honestly don't care if you just put my tools in some storage shed till they rust. Just promise me you will do one thing for me. Build a chair.
I love you son.
Dad.

Build a chair? What was that supposed to mean? I don't have the first clue about how to build a chair. Just then I look down at the chapter titles of the book I'm holding and laugh. '*Chapter*

8 All about chairs'. That's funny. As I page through chapter eight I see the chair I need to build. But this seems like a pretty big undertaking, especially for me. I read through the instructions and figure out what I need to buy to get started.

After dinner, I tell Sara that I'm going to clean up the old garage and she smiles. She's been asking me to do that for a while.

"Timing is everything, honey." I smile.

"Oh how I wish I controlled timing," she laughs.

"I bet you do," I say as I give her a kiss on the cheek.

Somewhere around 11 pm she comes out to the garage and finds me setting up my dad's tools.

"I thought you were going to clean out the garage?"

"Nope, I specifically said clean up."

"So, what is this about? Career change?" she asks wondering if this is a reason for concern.

"I don't think so. I think this is about finding some answers. But I'm not really sure. All I know is that I have to build a chair."

"Do you know how to do that?" she asks.

"Nope, no clue. All I know is that's what I need to do."

"Well, why don't you make me one?"

"No can do, everyone has to make their own chair," I say with a smile.

"Well, I don't know how to make a chair."

"I guess you'll have to figure it out then."

"Nice," she smiles. "Do you think this will help with... all your questions?"

She knows me enough by now, to know that if she pries too much before I'm ready to open up, it will just shut me down. So as much as she would love to lay out twenty questions in front of me, she steps gingerly into this conversation.

"I don't know. I'm not sure it's about that. I think it's about something more important than that."

"Ok, well don't be up too late."

"Thanks, Mom."

She smiles and shakes her head as she walks out of the garage and back toward the house.

Well, now that everything is set up I can start working on this chair I'm supposed to build. I look down at my watch. 1:30 am. Wow, I should get to bed.

Chapter 10

I find myself unmotivated at work today. I can't get this chair project off of my mind. When the clock finally strikes 5pm I'm out of that office as fast as I can. I stop by the hardware store on the way home and buy the wood I'll need for this project as well as some other supplies listed in the book.

As I walk into the house I find Sara in the kitchen cooking up another delicious meal.

"Hey, honey!"

"Hi," she says with a surprised tone. "I take it you're doing better."

"Yeah, I feel better."

"Great, how was work?"

"Same old, same old. But I couldn't get this chair project off of my mind. Are you ok with me working till dinner is ready?"

"Yeah, that's fine with me," she chuckles.

I change as quickly as I can out of my work clothes, and into work clothes. Isn't that funny. How work clothes can be so different depending on what you are working on.

I get to the shop and turn on the lights. As I sit down in the chair with my book I have the confidence of a woodworker who's spent his life shaping, crafting and creating, beauty.

Before dinner, I'm able to get the legs cut out. I shovel my food into my mouth quickly kiss the kids and Sara and head back out to the shop. I continue to follow the steps as best as I understand. Somewhere around step eight, I find myself a little confused. They're talking about rabbits and dovetails, and it's like I'm reading Chinese. I manage to get all the pieces cut out and laid out on the work table. I figure I can stain them tomorrow and then put them together over the weekend.

3 days later...

I can't say it's the most attractive chair I've ever seen, but I feel pretty good about it. Maybe this is what I needed. To excel in something. To prove to myself that I could do something well. Maybe I should start building chairs for people. I wonder how much money a woodworker makes? It's gotta be able to pay the bills, right?

I carry the chair into the house to show Sara and the kids what I've created. I call them all into the family room and let them gaze at my masterpiece.

They all look surprised. I think it's a good surprised. I can't really tell.

"Good job Dad," Lily says with a bit of hesitance in her voice.

"Babe, it looks great," Sara says affirming me.

"I know it's not the best looking chair ever, but it makes up for its looks by its sheer strength. This is a quality chair that will last for years."

At that, I sat firmly down in the chair to show them how strong it was.

"Crack!"

I find myself on the floor with tears welling up in my eyes. The pain in my body is superseded by the agony in my heart. I calmly stand up and pick up the pieces of the chair, hang my head and walk back toward the shop. I spend the next 5 minutes throwing pieces of the chair against the wall as I yell and cry.

"See! See! I'm not good at anything. You made a mistake when you made me." I cry out.

I didn't realize it at that point but there were years of anger toward God that were being unleashed in that moment. And the worst part. There was no answer on the other end of the line.

About an hour later Sara shows up at the door to find me slumped down in an old office chair, with pieces of broken wood strewn about and the book over in the corner next to the trashcan.

"Babe?" she says calmly as she walks into the garage.

"I don't really want to talk."

"That's ok, I just wanted to tell you that I'm really proud of you. I know things didn't work out the way that you expected, but you tried and you really did build a good chair."

"All my life has been like that chair," I say with discouragement overtaking my words. "What am I, Sara? And don't you dare say I'm a child of God. What father treats His kid like this? Those pat answers don't work in my life. I can tell you anything you want to know about God, and I don't have a clue who He is...." I pause and take a breath. "If He is," I mumble.

"What?" she says with an overwhelming tone of sadness. "Are you doubting God? Lewis, you can't. What about all our years of following Him?"

"Following Him?" I say with scorn. "You call going to a meeting and reading a book and talking into space, following Him? People follow the Grateful Dead, more than we follow God. Sara, I'm really sorry, I don't mean to make you walk through any of this. But I don't know that I can confidently say that I believe anymore."

"Lewis, please. Don't give up on all this," she says now pleading with me.

"Sara, I won't stop you from going to church or doing all those things that make you feel okay with God. But, please just let me be."

There was nothing for her to say in this moment. With tears streaming down her face she turned and left.

I spent another hour sitting there trying to plan out what I was going to do with my extra time since I wasn't going to be attending church anymore. But nothing really seemed attractive to me. Finally, I decided I would figure it out in the morning. As I walked back toward the house I saw my camp chair once again sitting in the middle of the yard. That's it, there's going to be a punishment for them if they can't put my stuff away. As I grabbed the chair I felt that same feeling. Something tugging on me to sit down right here in the middle of the yard. Yeah right, I'm going to bed.

Chapter 11

I wake up feeling like I have a hangover, but I didn't have any alcohol. Sara is in the bathroom getting ready. I can hear her crying and mumbling.

"You okay, Honey?" I say from the bed.

"Yeah, yeah I'm fine. Just running late for church."

"Oh, well I can get breakfast ready for you guys if you want?"

At this she started crying harder. Church had been such a stabilizing force in her life. It was like the thing that made her feel like everything was ok and would be ok. I used to feel like that too. But not anymore.

I head downstairs to make some eggs and bacon.

"This is great," Sammy says as he and Lily walk into the kitchen. "We don't normally have time for this kind of breakfast on Sundays. What made you decide to make a big breakfast Dad?"

"Well, I'm gonna stay home today Sammy, so I figured I could make you guys a big breakfast."

"Are you sick Dad?"

"Nope, just have some stuff to work on here."

"Sweet, can I stay home too?"

"Sorry Sammy, you and Lily still need to go with Mom to church."

"But why Dad?"

At this Sara walked in the kitchen.

"Here Honey, here's your plate," I said as I handed it to her.

"No thanks, Lewis, I'm not really hungry."

"Mom, are you sick? Cause if you're sick, then we definitely don't have to go to church," said Sammy.

"Sammy, we are going to church," she said as she sent a glare in my direction. "Your father just needs to stay home to work on some things."

Wisdom in this situation says, 'keep your mouth shut'. I try to listen to wisdom when it stumbles into my mind. I realize that, in this moment, I can't make her happy. Making her happy will actually cause me to be fake in this situation.

They leave and I'm left to the relaxing chore of cleaning up the kitchen. Something about hand-washing dishes calms me down. After I'm finished cleaning I walk over to the couch and sit down. I think about turning on the t.v. but have no desire to watch anything.

I feel better after sleeping last night, but there's still a sting in my heart. I find myself talking out loud. As if God can hear me better when I talk out loud. I'm asking questions. Questions that I have carried like weights in a backpack for years now. Questions that were never addressed and couldn't be answered inside the walls of that church. Questions no man could figure out for me. Questions that not even my wife, who knew me better than anyone, was able to solve.

"God, what is the point of any of this?" I know that's a broad question. "How about why do I go to church and feel filled up for a day and then return to the same life of frustration and questions soon after. Or how about this one, Why are you late sometimes? Why does it seem like there's never enough? Why is it that, I've lived my life going to church and helping people, reading my bible and praying, and my life has always felt like it's missing something?"

I sit there for the next five minutes in the silence. I laugh out loud. "Now this feels like what I'm used to. Your silence in response to my need."

I stand up and walk out the back door. As I look over at the shop I remember that I left my favorite coffee cup on the work table. I walk inside and into the still looming frustration from my breakdown the day before. I decide to pick up the pieces of broken wood strewn across the floor and place them on the work table. Most of it is useless and shattered, but there are a few pieces that could be reused. No! what I am saying? I'm not touching this stuff again.

I walk over to pick up a piece of wood that's in the corner and see the book laying there with the back cover opened. I can see there's another note from my dad. I pick up the book and begin to read.

P.S.

Lewis, excitement and zeal aren't what makes good craftsmanship. You have to be willing to take your time with each cut. You have to understand how things fit together before you glue them, and sanding is an art in and of itself. Take your time Lewis, and if you need to fix something or rebuild something, it isn't a failure, it's learning.

Trust me when I tell you that building this chair will open up doors for you. But make sure you build it the right way. It's not only about the finished product. It's about your care for each step.

He always knew what to say when he was alive. Apparently he still does. I stand there shaking my head. I take a deep breath and decide that maybe giving it another shot wouldn't be the worst decision.

I walk inside to grab some coffee and head back out to my woodshop. I decide to start calling it my woodshop. Who knows maybe it will add to the property value. I sit down on the old office chair and wheel myself over to the work table. I open the book and begin to read chapter 8 again. I finish as Sara pulls in the driveway. I now have an idea of how all this works, but I'm still not sure I could actually build something that doesn't fall apart. I close the book and head into the house. I can tell I feel a little better but I'm trying not to show it too much, knowing that Sara wants me to feel bad for not going to church with her.

"Hi Honey, how was church?"

"It was fine. If you are that interested you can listen to the sermon online."

"That's ok, I'm sure it was a good one," I say. I know what game she's playing. I plan on volleying these shots right back to her. She's not happy with that one. "Come on Sara, how long are you going to be mad at me?" I laugh, trying to ease the tension.

"Lewis, I don't understand you. I don't understand how you can lay aside all that we've believed in just because you don't have answers for everything. I'm not mad at you, I just don't get you, and honestly, I feel like I don't know you anymore."

"You mean since last night?" I probably could have held that one in, but I'm trying to ward off the heaviness that she's putting on me right now, and humor seems like a good shield.

"Ughh!"

Yep, should've kept that in. She walks out of the kitchen and toward our bedroom.

"Hey guys, how was church?" I say to Sammy and Lily.

"Good dad. We learned about God, Jesus, and the Bible." Sammy says with sarcasm.

I knew how he felt, I wanted to start ranting right then about how I felt and how it didn't seem like people were getting any real change for their lives in church. But again, my friend Wisdom whispered in my ear, and I decided to listen.

"Sammy, there's got to be something good about going to church. Right?"

"Well, other than the cute new girl, I can't think of any."

"Alright."

"Dad?" says Lily. "Mom says you don't like God anymore and you think church is bad. Is that true?"

"Ha, Lily" I say with a smile. "Dad is working through some things in his life right now. I didn't say any of those things. I just have a lot of questions right now."

"Ok, Daddy. But you aren't going to leave us are you?"

"No sweetie, why would you say that?"

"Well, you know Jeremy, my friend from church?"

"Yeah"

"His dad stopped going to church and then moved away to another state."

"Sweetie, I'm not going anywhere. I just need to find some answers that I haven't been able to figure out from where I've been."

"Ok Daddy," she says as she walks out of the kitchen.

Chapter 12

The next few weeks seem to be a blur. We fall into a new routine, and although I know Sara isn't happy with me, she's at least not giving me the cold shoulder like she was before. We actually had a really good talk last night about all of this that I'm working through, and for the first time I felt like she was actually able to hear what I was trying to communicate.

Here I am again in the silence of the house on a Sunday morning. I decide to head back out to the woodshop to work on my new project. I spent the last three weeks building little things, like a jewelry box for Lily and a wooden squirrel who's tail can pull out a hot oven rack. Now that was a good idea. I wouldn't say I'm a craftsman yet, but I'm starting to understand some things about how to put stuff together and I'm finding that I feel more at peace in life than I had before. Although I know a part of me is dying, I can tell there are other parts that are being brought to life. Before I would feel like I needed to keep up a persona of having things together. From my clothes, to our cars, to our family. I really put a lot of stock in keeping those things in good appearance to others, but now I don't really care about any of that.

I look across the yard as I get to the woodshop and see my camp chair. Are you serious? I really need to talk to them about this. It's not even like they are leaving their own stuff out in the yard. I walk over to put it away once again, and that feeling hits me. "Fine, I'll sit down," I say out loud.

As I sit down everything begins to spin in my head. And in an instant I find myself sitting in the middle of this field with rocks strewn throughout, it is cold and lifeless. A fog has settled and although there a few trees, even they look as though they constantly live in the dead of winter. I look around and see a rock wall surrounding me. The wind is blowing hard against me. Feelings of panic overwhelm me so strongly that I fall forward, throwing myself out of the chair and onto the grass in my back yard. I look up and take note of everything that's around me. There's the woodshop, there's the maple tree, there's the trampoline. Ok, I'm okay. I take a deep breath and sit up. I stare at the chair for about a minute. What was that? It must have been the jelly doughnut I had for breakfast. Bad idea. I carefully fold up the chair trying not to get it too close to my body. I walk it back to the house and set it against the siding.

I then head back to the woodshop but keep looking back at it as I'm walking. I shake my head as I turn on the lights and get ready to start building my next project, cup holders.

1 hour later...

"Hi Babe," Sara says as she walks in my woodshop.
"Uh, honey..."
"Oh that's right, I'm sorry babe. Hello Master Carpenter!"
"Much better," I smile as she walks toward me and wraps her arms around me.
"How was it?" I ask.
"Good, it was encouraging."
"That's great."
"Listen, this isn't me hassling you, I just had a thought."
"Go ahead."
"Would you consider meeting with Pastor Tom and just sharing what you're going through with him?"
At first, I feel this thing rise up in me, but I have this different thought that overrides that one. What could it hurt?
"Sure honey, I'll give him a call this week."
"Really, you will?"
"Yeah, it can't hurt to talk, right?"

"Uh, right." She squeezes me again and then turns to head back to the house. "Hey babe?"

"Yeah?" I say.

"I would like to have one of those cup holders when they're finished. I think they are beautiful," she says with a smile.

"Thanks, honey, you got it."

I'm not really sure how Pastor Tom could help. I mean I highly doubt he's ever had questions like this, but maybe he'll be able to give me some direction. I know my dad always loved him. He and my dad would get coffee about once a month and my dad would always tell me about how there were pastors, and then there were shepherds, and Pastor Tom was a shepherd. At the funeral Pastor Tom came up to me and hugged me and told me if I ever needed anything to just ask. I never took him up on that offer. I'm not really sure that he has anything I need, but we'll see.

Chapter 13

Days later…

"Hi Pastor Tom, thanks for meeting with me."

"Of course, Lewis. I was actually glad to hear that you set up this meeting. I've missed seeing you at church."

"Yeah, I uh, well…"

"Listen, Lewis. I'm not your priest, I'm your pastor. There's a big difference between those two roles. You don't have to apologize to me or feel bad about not coming to a service."

"Oh, ok, thanks."

"So, what is it that you wanted to talk about?"

"Well, I guess I'm just struggling with all the years I've spent in church and feeling like it doesn't match up to what my life looks like. You know if you work forty hours in a week you get forty hours a week of pay. But with God, it seems like I'm not earning what I've worked for. I'm sorry if that sounds bad, I just…"

"Lewis, you don't have to apologize. Listen, I've gone through my own season of questions and confusion."

"You have?"

"Actually it was about ten years ago."

"Wait, was that when you went on vacation for a few months?"

"Yeah, they call it a sabbatical. It's a fancy word for forgetting why you are doing what you're doing and needing to unplug and regain perspective. Anyway, I think I understand some of what you are feeling."

"Wow, I never thought a pastor would struggle with any of this."

"Yeah, we actually are more human than you would think," he says with a smile. "Go on, tell me about your questions."

I spend the next hour sharing all of what's going on inside my head, as he laughs and recounts his own stories and questions.

After I finish he sits forward in his chair and looks me in the eye the way my father used to.

"Lewis, sometimes when we are walking away from all that we know, we actually find ourselves on the path we are supposed to be on."

"I don't feel like I'm closer to anything though," I say.

"You know how most parents send their kids to school not just for education, but hoping that the school system will also teach them some form of obedience and character."

"Yeah, Sara and I were talking about that last week."

"Well, I think a lot of people view church that way. They come to church hoping that the church will build their house for them. But it was never intended to be that way. The church is only here to help you make sure your foundation is true and strong. But the house, that's for you and Jesus to build."

"I don't feel like I even know Jesus anymore."

"I know that feeling all too well."

"Really?"

"Yeah, really. There's been times before I get up to preach, that I question if I really believe all that I'm about to say. Sometimes it's the devil, but sometimes it's a room in my house that hasn't been finished. It's a place in my heart that Jesus is showing me still needs some attention. I'm confident you'll figure it out. I don't know what that will look like, but I'm sure you'll know it when it happens."

"Ok, thanks for your time," I say as I stand up to leave.

"Lewis."

"Yeah Pastor?"

"Don't believe that your attendance at a church service will appease people or God. He's after your heart, anything less won't do."

"Thanks," I said as I walked out of the office.

Well, that went way different than I expected it to. I can't wait to share that with Sara.

30 minutes later…

"Hi Honey," I say as I walk in the door.

"Hey there," she says as she walks over and wraps her arms around me. "How did it go? Did he answer your questions?"

"Actually, no. He sort of just listened."

"Really?"

I could hear the disappointment in her voice. I knew that she was hoping this meeting would change me back to what I was. She didn't realize that I couldn't go back there. It looked like I was just hanging out in space with no clear answer as to where I was headed, but I felt more confident now, that something was happening. Unfortunately for her, all of it felt out of control.

"But I did gain some good perspective from our talk." I say trying to help her understand it was a helpful thing.

"Like what?"

"Well, I don't think this is too big of a deal, you know, all my questions. I think maybe I have to walk through this, like it's actually a part of my journey."

"Seriously Lewis? I mean I've tried to stay calm, I've tried to give you space, and I've tried to keep my mouth closed, but how do I know you're not going to go off and cheat on me or become a raging alcoholic? The church is like a safe place, and you are walking away from all that safety, and you want me to just stand by and be okay with all the implications of this? I don't think I can do that."

Every time she loses it like this I feel it deep in my heart. I would do anything to make her happy. Lord knows I have tried throughout our marriage, but she doesn't realize what she's asking of me, well, what she's trying to force me into, I should say.

"Nope," I respond looking down at the ground.

"Nope? What do you mean Nope? Lewis, this is serious, can you not see that? Please answer me," she said with a raised tone.

"I mean, nope, I don't expect you to feel okay about it. I only have one request in this." I pause and look up into her eyes. "Please love me the way you think your Jesus would."

Tears welled up in her eyes. She threw the towel down on the counter that she had been holding in her hand and walked, crying, to our bedroom.

I knew this was so hard for her to walk through feeling like she was losing me and not sure where I was going to land, but that was her part of this journey to deal with, not mine. No matter how hard I tried I couldn't make this easier for her. Her dad had left her and her mom when she was twelve years old. They had always gone to church as a family. But one day the truth came out that he had another life and then he was gone. There was a deep wound in her heart from that, and I knew that she always wondered if I would someday do the same thing. I understand her pain, but in some ways, this situation might be just what she needs to be healed and to learn to trust again.

Chapter 14

The next day…

"Hi honey," she says as she walks into my woodshop.

"Oh, hey there," I say as I slide the cupholder I've been working on for her under some other pieces of wood. I turn to see the sadness still lingering in her eyes from last night.

"Are you ready to come in for dinner?"

"Yeah, I'll be there in five minutes."

"Ok, I'll see you then," she says awkwardly.

I know there is so much that she wants to say in this moment. She really wants to open up the bag of hurt and confusion that she didn't find resolution to last night, but I think she realizes where it will lead us right now.

I finish up the cupholder, wipe it down with a rag, and smile. This is satisfying.

Work has become more bearable with having this as an outlet. It's like now that I have something filling me up outside of work, it doesn't seem to drag me down as much.

"Hey Sara, come here," I motion to her as I walk toward the table.

"Yeah what is it?"

"I made this for you," I say as I hand her the cupholder.

She looks down and reads the inscription that was burned into the wood.

'I will always be there to hold you up and catch your tears. -Love Lewis"

She chuckles and smiles. "Wow, even with all of the mean things I said to you, you still make this for me? What is changing you, Lewis?"

"I'm not exactly sure. I just think for so much of my life I was on the path that everyone else told me was a good one, and it feels like for the first time I'm on the right one for me. I actually like my life right now, and surprising as it may seem I like you too, even after what you said to me," I say with a big smile.

"Nice," she says as she hits me in the arm, and then looks back down at her cupholder. "Well, I'm sorry, I'm just scared and I tend to fight when I'm scared."

"I know, and I forgive you."

"Thank you," she says as she moves into my open arms and puts her head against my chest.

As she pulls away she wipes her tears on her sleeve and walks to the stairs to call the kids down for dinner.

"Go get washed up Lewis."

"Yes, ma'am."

Later that night...

"Honey, I'm gonna go to bed early. I'm just really tired tonight," she says as she walks by me at the table. "Are you gonna watch your show? It should be on in five minutes."

"Oh really? Nah, I don't think so. I might just go work for a little bit in the shop."

"You really do love being out there don't you? Do you think it's because it reminds you of your dad?"

"I'm sure that's a part of it, but honestly, I think there's something more to it, I'm just not sure what yet."

"Well, I hope you figure it all out before Jesus returns."

"Oh Sara," I say as I laugh and take her in my arms. "I think this is just a part of me that I never knew existed. And it's actually making all of my life feel more full than before."

"Ok, well I'm glad for you, I'm just still a little worried."

"I hear that worrying is a sin," I joke.

"You…"

"So is name-calling and bad words," I sneak in before she finishes her sentence.

She just shakes her head and snuggles into my embrace.

"I love you," I whisper.

She loosens all the tension in her body.

"I love you too, goodnight."

As I walk out toward the shop, I again see that chair sitting in the middle of the yard. Every time I see it there the kids are already asleep. I really need to figure out who keeps leaving it there. After the last situation, I'm trying to stay away from it. I head straight to the shop to start working on a squirrel oven rack puller for Shirley, a lady at the church who heard about them and begged Sara to have me make her one.

I begin to cut out the drawing of the squirrel with my dad's old scroll saw. Somewhere around the ears, I hear someone out in the yard say my name. I shut off the saw and walk around the corner. No one's there.

I keep working and hear it again a minute later. Again I shut off the saw and walk out into the yard. No one.

"Hello? Did someone call me?"

I look around the yard but don't see anything or anyone. Just that chair, staring at me as if it's some sort of an invitation.

"I don't think so," I say out loud as I turn to go back into the shop. Just then I hear it again, 'Lewis', but I can't hear it in my ears. It's somehow inside of me.

This is too strange, I think. Everything in me wants to go back into the shop and keep working, but this pull toward that chair is really intriguing to me.

"Fine, I'll sit in the chair," I say as I throw my hands up in the air and walk toward the middle of the yard.

I walk around it one time and put my hand on the back of it. I'm still here, good. I walk to the front of it and slowly sit down. I stop just before my backside hits the fabric of the chair.

"Good, it must have just been in my head last time," I mumble.

I sit back and relax my body into the chair. WHAM!!!

It feels like the wind was knocked out of me. I gasp, feeling as if this is the only natural response, but soon realize that I have more than enough air. My eyes take a second to adjust, but even then I can see very little due to an intense fog surrounding me. I can't make much out. But there's a figure walking toward me. I'm not sure whether to be terrified or glad by this visitor. When he is about 20 feet away from me the fog is pushed away in an instant, as if a strong wind had blown it from in between us. Immediately my eyes are overwhelmed by the view that surrounds us. I am sitting on the top of a large mountain. As far as I can see it is just mountains, beautiful green, lush mountains. There is a pile of rocks over to my right. He sits down right in front of me, dressed in some outfit that looks like it's from the Middle East.

"Hello Lewis."

"Hi," I say hesitantly.

"Welcome."

"Thank you, but how? I mean, who? I mean, I don't know."

"I know there are many questions going through your mind right now. For now, know this. My name is Ammoris. As far as your question of how, because this is truth. And as for the why? Because you are ready. You sat in the chair and your journey has led you to the place where your heart was open to receive. Some would call it the place of 'surrender'."

"Listen, Ammoris, right? My wife just told me that she was worried about me slipping off the deep end. This is really going to throw a wrench in our marriage. Can I just go back to the chair in my yard? I mean I don't know how I can even explain this to anyone, let alone her."

He sighs and smiles. "You always had good wit. Unfortunately, you can't return to the knowledge of before this visit, but yes you can go back to the chair in your mind."

"What do you mean in my mind? This is in my mind. That chair is my reality, that chair has substance, this feels like I'm in a cloud, and by the way, how do you know me?"

"Yes, it would to you. Oh, Lewis. There is much I need to teach you and show you, but I would rather this visit be between two old friends than a teacher and his student."

"Whoa, whoa, whoa. I need to sign up for classes before I'm a student, and not sure if you saw this or not, but I never signed my name on the attendance sheet."

"Hahaha," he laughs with a laugh from deep within. "Fair enough, then let us just talk as friends. So, what has it been like for you?"

"What do you mean?" I say still very hesitant with this guy. I'm still trying to figure out why he feels like we are friends, and I have no recollection of him at all.

"Your life? What has it been like for you? Have you enjoyed it?"

"Well, I guess not really, up until the last few months. I've always felt unsatisfied and unfulfilled, but something changed in the last few months."

"You mean after you read your dad's note in the book?"

"What? That's it, who are you? Do you have camera's in my house? Is this The Matrix?"

"Oh Lewis, you make me laugh. Let's just say I knew you before you were Lewis. I knew you then like a friend."

"How come I don't remember you?"

"It is the way it must be," he says as he smiles sincerely. "But, you are here now, and it is time for us to regain what has been stolen from you all those years."

"Ok, well. Yeah, it was after the note in the book my dad gave to me. After that, I sort of felt like life had meaning. And now I'm actually enjoying it."

"I see. Well, then it is a good season, that needed to come about in your life."

"Yeah, that's what I'm trying to communicate to Sara, my wife, but she doesn't seem to get it."

"As would no one who hasn't taken that journey, or sat in that chair," he says as he smiles.

I nod and smile. "Ammoris? What is this place?"

"Think of it as a place between. You are neither here nor there, just somewhere in between."

"Wow, that was the most confusing statement I think I've ever heard."

"Hahaha," he laughs. "Yes, but if you continue to visit me here, you will understand."

"So, I can come back here?"

"Yes, you can, but it is not by your will or determination. Only by your surrender. Do you have any other questions?" He says.

"A million, and yet none I can think of at this moment."

"Process requires time, don't despise time Lewis, it is the foundation of your world. For some, time only takes and steals, but for others, each second is like a stepping stone they are invited to walk on. You get to decide which person you will be."

"Ok," I say, taking a deep breath. "Hey, what is that in your hand?"

"These are precious stones. Do you remember them?"

"Yes," I say hesitantly. "My dream. Those are the jewels."

"Do you remember them from before your dream?"

"No, I don't."

"It's okay. In moments spent here you may. Well, I'm afraid you must be going now," he says.

"Already? I sure would love to stay for a little while longer."

"I know son, but our visits are on purpose, every detail of them strategically designed."

"Ok, well I'll come back tomorrow. I'll see you then."

He chuckles as he reaches over and waves his hand over my eyes.

I wake up into the chair in my backyard and feel a peace wash over me like I haven't felt before in my life.

I sit there for at least five more minutes as my mind paces back and forth between the possibility of this actually happening and everything I experienced.

As I head into the house I keep looking back at the chair, wondering what in the world just happened to me.

I fall asleep and rest as if nothing bad has ever happened to me in my whole lifetime. It was a sweet and deep sleep.

Chapter 15

I'm honestly having a tough time paying attention at work today. How do you experience something that literally disconnects you from your reality, and then go back into what was normal? I'm still unsure of how to tell this to anyone, especially Sara. I mean she's already worried about me and I don't think she could possibly understand any of this. I'm not exactly sure that I understand it. I just know that for the first time since I can remember, I felt at peace.

"Oh no," I say as I look at the clock. I need to meet a potential client in 10 minutes. I grab my bag and coat and walk out of my office.

15 minutes later…

"Hi, Luke?" I say as I hold out my hand to the man sitting at a corner table in the bistro downtown.

"Hey, Lewis right?" He says as he stands up and shakes my hand.

"I'm sorry I'm late."

"No problem at all, have a seat. I think the waitress will be right back to take our order."

"Ok great," I say as I scan the menu.

I'm not even sure that I'm hungry. I have this client in front of me and if he signs our contract this will an incredible opportunity for our company and for me, and all my brain wants to do is go back to last night.

The waitress comes by and takes our order.

Luke orders a grilled chicken salad and I choose the All American Cheeseburger and fries.

"So, Luke tell me about any concerns you have about us working together?"

"Well, that's a great question," he goes on for the next few minutes explaining his company's needs and direction. He doesn't seem to have any concerns but asks a couple of times about who will be managing the account.

The waitress brings our food to the table and I begin to eat as he continues talking.

I'm trying so hard to stay focused but just can't seem to concentrate.

"Yeah, that all sounds great, I mean except the bad stuff of course," I laugh. "And in answer to your question, I'll be handling the account personally. Did you have a chance to look over the proposal I sent you last week?"

"Yes, I did, thank you. It looked pretty good to me. Seems to cover all the bases. I have a couple of addendums, but nothing major, just loose ends that's all. I'll send it back in the morning. Thanks again for meeting with me, I just really like to meet in person whoever I'm going to be working with. As far as I'm concerned we're good to go."

"Oh, wow. That's great. Thank you. We will do our best."

"I know you will, Lewis. So, tell me about your life," he says as he starts eating.

"Oh, well. I have a son and a daughter. My son loves sports and my daughter loves to dance and play in the mud," I laugh as I think about the dichotomy that is my little angel. "My wife is, well, amazing. She does a lot and has walked through a lot with me. After college, I was really spinning my wheels trying to find out what to do in life. I was working at a retail store and just not getting anywhere. And then a friend helped me out, and since then we've been doing a lot better.

"Wow, that's great. Are you content?"

"What do you mean?"

"You know, are you satisfied with life?" He says as he shoves in a mouthful of lettuce. "Or do you always feel like you're missing something?" He mumbles while chewing.

"Well, up until a couple of months ago, I probably would've said I wasn't satisfied. Even now, I'm not sure that I am but I at least feel like I have more of an outlet."

"Cool, what's that?"

"What's what?"

"Your outlet? You said you found an outlet?"

"Oh, yeah. It's uh, well, I guess it's carpentry. My dad was a carpenter, and when he passed he left me all of his tools. Well, they were in this storage building out back of our house for years. But just recently, I found this book he gave me awhile back. I opened it and found a note that he had written to me. I never knew it was there. It was really helpful, and so I started making stuff. Nothing major, just little things."

"Wow, that's great. Have you made a chair yet?"

"Ha. Have you talked to my wife?"

"No, why?"

"Oh, nothing. I tried to make a chair, but it fell apart and well, it just wasn't a good experience."

"I see. Well, can I be really honest with you Lewis."

"Yeah, sure."

"So, in the morning I walk in the woods and it's like this special time for me and God. We talk about all sorts of things, but sometimes we just walk and don't talk at all. It's just really special. Well anyway, this morning I was walking and we were talking, and He brought up my meeting with you. He told me that you needed to build a chair. I thought it sounded crazy myself, but I decided to ask why. Do you know what he said?"

"Uh, no. I have no idea," I say completely enthralled with this conversation.

"He said, the chair is your gate. Any thoughts on that one?"

"No, no clue. It doesn't make much sense to me at all."

"Well, think about it. What is a gate?" He says as he takes another bite of food.

"It's uh, like a door I guess."

"Yeah, but it's more than a door. It's an opening, it's the way to get into something. Maybe God is inviting you to sit down."

"I sit down for 8 hours a day at work."

"Yeah, I know," he laughs. "But this isn't about sitting down, it's about the posture of your heart. It's about finding a place of rest and waiting there. I honestly get the sense that the chair is like a portal to another realm for you."

"Does any of that fit or make sense?"

I sigh deeply wondering if I can really tell this guy what happened last night. I mean, this could blow the sale if he thinks I'm crazy. But, who else could I tell?

"Yeah, it does," I say as I look down at my food.

"Haha, well tell me about it, Lewis. I didn't get the whole story from God this morning, but I sure would love to hear from you," he says as he wipes his mouth with his napkin and sits back against his chair.

"This is gonna sound crazy."

"Even better," he says with a smile.

"So, my camp chair kept getting left out in the back of our yard. I thought it was my kids. But now I don't think it was them. The first couple of times I saw it, I felt this draw to sit in it, but I didn't do it. I just picked it up and put it away. The first time I sat in it, I was immediately in this other place, but I freaked out and threw myself out of the chair. Last night it was out again and so I sat down in it and had this crazy experience. This guy named Ammoris was there and he was telling me all sorts of stuff. I honestly don't know what to make of all of it. All I know is that I've lived most of my life looking for the next thing that would hopefully fill me up in some way, but never did. Last night, I felt like I was so full I would explode. I wanted nothing else than to stay right where I was."

"Wow!" He says as he leans forward. "Man, Lewis, that's incredible. Dude, do you know what you just did?"

"No clue whatsoever."

He chuckles, "Lewis you got to sit with Jesus and talk with Him. How amazing is that? You definitely need to build a chair."

"Why is that?"

"Because He's telling you to. That's the only reason you'll ever need to do the things He's asking you to do."

"Alright, I'll think about it."

"Lewis, I'm so glad we got to meet. Listen I gotta run to another meeting, but we'll be in touch, and maybe we can grab lunch again in a month or so."

"Yeah, that would be great. Thank you. For talking and all."

"You're welcome," he says with a sincere smile as he turns to leave.   "Send me a picture of that chair when you finish it," he says as he walks away.

"Ha, okay. I will," I say as I lean back in my chair.

As I head back to work I find myself conflicted over whether or not I should tell Sara. I mean, if anybody would love me for who I am, it's her. But on the other hand, this is pretty out there.

Chapter 16

"Hey Dad," Sam says as I walk in through the side door.

"Hey Sam, how was your day?"

"It was pretty good. Nothing too special. Hey Dad?"

"Yeah, what's up."

"I got up to go to the bathroom last night and I saw you sitting in the chair in the backyard. Are you ok?"

"Oh, um yeah. I'm great. What did it look like?" I ask wondering if it looked to him like it felt to me.

"Uh, it looked like you were sitting in a chair, in the backyard, late at night. It was a little weird."

"Haha, yeah. It must've looked kind of weird. I was just... trying to relax and you know, chill out a little bit."

"Dad? You're not doing drugs are you?"

"No! Why would you think that?"

"I don't know, you're just acting kind of strange lately, with all the time you're spending in the shed."

"Uh, it's actually a workshop, Son," I interrupt.

"Right, the workshop. Anyways, with all that and you zoning last night. I'm just worried about you."

"Well, thank you for your concern. But I can assure you that I'm doing fine. You know Sam, a lot of life is like a journey. Sometimes we forget that it's like that and we get stuck in just surviving here, or trying to get everything we think will make us happy. I'm going through a time in my life where I'm starting to figure some of that out."

"You mean like a midlife crisis?"

"I don't think it's that, but where did you hear that?"

"Oh Tommy's dad went through one last year. He bought a motorcycle and cut his hair short and spiky. He even started wearing clothes that teenagers wear."

"No, then not like that at all. See, I like my haircut, and I don't know if you know this, but my mustache is a sign of honor that is dated back to the beginning of time."

Just then Sara peaks her head around the corner, "So, it's like ancient history, the mustache that is?"

"Very nice, dear," I respond as she and Sam laugh.

"How was your day, honey?" I say as she walks in to greet me.

"It was good, how was yours?"

"Interesting."

"Oh yeah, how so?"

"I met a really interesting client for lunch. It made me really think about some stuff. Oh yeah, and that big account I was telling you about. I'm pretty sure we got it. Actually that was the client I met."

"Oh that's great babe. I'm so happy for you."

"Thanks, me too. Hopefully that gets James off my back for a little while."

"So, what was it that was so interesting about your meeting?"

"Well, I..." I pause not sure how much I should share. "I guess he was just really encouraging in the things of life that actually matter. You know he seems to be a Christian. At least he talks like it. He says he goes for walks in the morning and talks with God. And it seems like God talks back to him. It all sounds a little crazy to me, but maybe that works for some people."

"Well, don't you think if God talked to some people He would talk to all of us? I mean what's special about him?"

"I don't know Sara. Maybe it works differently than we've understood. Maybe we've just been ignorant."

"I don't know about you, Lewis, but I'm not ignorant. I've gone to church since I was a girl. I know all the things about God. I think I would know about this too. If God hadn't given us the Bible, then maybe we should expect Him to speak to us. But, we don't need to hear from Him like that anymore. He gave us everything we needed to know in His book. That's enough for me, and I feel like I've got things pretty well figured out."

At this point Sam gets up, and gives us both the look of, 'this probably isn't going to end well', and walks to his room.

"Well, not me. I feel like I'm standing on the edge of the Grand Canyon and all the vastness before me is the knowledge of God, and I don't have a clue where to begin."

"I know you don't want to hear this, but maybe you could begin by going back to church?"

"Sara…. Never mind."

"No, say it. I've been dying to understand you, so in the moment when you are finally going to lay it all out there for me, please don't hold back," she says showing more of her increasing agitation.

"Fine. I sat in a chair in the backyard late last night," I say very matter of factly, "and the moment I sat down I was in another world. And there was a man there, whose name is Ammoris, and he told me a whole lot of things about my life. This client today, told me that Jesus was meeting with me and this was a special thing, and I believe him," I paused and looked up into her eyes waiting to hear what blast from the cannon would come next. But, nothing came. She just stood there for 10 seconds. It seemed like an eternity as I waited for some sort of response. And then like a dam that was breaking loose, she started to cry. First slowly than uncontrollably, until finally she turned and ran to our room. She slammed the door and fell on our bed.

I walked to the door and whispered through it.

"I'm not sure why that hurt you so much. I'm sorry that it did. But I can't change what is happening to me, and honestly Sara, I don't want to. It's a good thing that's happening. I feel more alive than ever. I feel like there is purpose to me being here."

"It feels to me like I'm losing you, Lewis," she manages to get out between sobs. "It feels like you're changing from what made us work so well together, and that I have to be the stable one in the relationship."

"I'm sorry, Sara. I'll be out in the shop."

She continues to sob as I leave.

As I sit down in the old office chair. I decide to again read back through the chapter on building a chair. As I read I realize there are 2 pages that are stuck together that I hadn't noticed before. I pry them apart and begin to read. It's all about cross support pieces between the legs.

"That's why my chair didn't work!" I say out loud.

I keep reading as I begin to understand how important this is to the structure of the chair. And in that moment as I am thinking about how my first chair fell apart, I ponder how it feels the same for Sara and I right now. I'm not sure how I can help her. I feel like if I stop the direction I'm being led, then life isn't worth living, but if I keep going and even try to be open with her about it, I feel like we'll never be connected.

"Ammoris?" I say quietly. "If you're really Jesus like Luke says you are, can you help me with Sara? How do I love her through all of this?"

Just then Sara walks through the door holding a balled up tissue and still working out the last of her tears.

"Oh, hey honey, I was just..."

"Talking to yourself. It just keeps getting better," she says smiling through her tears.

"I was actually talking to... God."

"Oh, well, that's good, but which god?"

"Haha, nice one. The same one that made you and your snarky attitude," I say with a laugh.

She just shakes her head as she walks over to me and sits down in my lap.

"I'm sorry. I don't understand you or what is happening, but I love you. Please just don't shut me out."

"Deal," I say as I wrap my arms around her. "Hey, by the way," I say. "I think I'm going to build another chair."

"I think that's a great idea."

"Really, why is that?"

"You fell off the horse, Lewis. What else is there to do but to get back on?"

"Thanks, Babe."

Chapter 17

Later that same day...

"Goodnight Sara," I say as I walk through the kitchen. "I'll be out at the shop."
"Ok honey. Just don't be up too late."
"You got it."
I head out to the shop and start the cutout for the seat of the chair. As I finish up sanding the edges I notice our bedroom light turn off. Sara must be in bed. I decide to go meet my new friend. The camp chair is leaning against the house. I grab it and set it up in the same place it was. I take a deep breath and sit down. I feel the coolness of the fabric through my shirt as I settle back.

Just then I have a strange feeling that nothing is happening. I stand up turn to look at the chair, then sit back down. Still nothing. This is weird, I think. I try rocking back into the chair a little bit harder. "Maybe it's just that I'm not hitting the contact points?" I say. "Contact points, haha? What am I saying. This is ridiculous. Maybe it was all made up?"

A dread comes over me. What if none of that was real? For the first time I can remember I felt like life was on purpose and like I was supposed to be here for a reason, and if that was all made up, then what do I have left?

I sit there with my head in my hands and start to cry.

"Ammoris? If you're not real, if none of this was real, can you please just tell me? Haha, you idiot. If he's not real, then how would he answer me?" I say laughing at myself. "Maybe it's just not working tonight," I say as I sit back.

Just then I remember the end of our conversation last night. And I realize, I may not be able to come back whenever I want to.

I spend the next 20 minutes reliving my time with him last night. All the feelings I experienced, all the beauty that surrounded us, and as much as I could remember from what he said. And I decide in that moment to count it a blessing no matter what else happens.

I stand up and start walking to the house.

About halfway between the chair and the house I hear it. That voice inside of me telling me to go sit down in the chair.

I don't know about this, I think. I stop and turn to look at the chair. My mind begins to go back and forth.

But what if nothing happens. Then I'll have wasted my time and I'll feel like a fool.

I should get to bed so I'm not exhausted at work tomorrow.

I was just in the chair, how can 1 minute make a difference?

And as these thoughts like arrows fly through my mind I become weary from just thinking about it and decide to go to bed.

The next day...

"Hey Lewis, great job on landing that account.," says James as he walks by my office.

"Oh, thanks James. Yeah, it went really smoothly."

"Good, hey listen I uh, need to tell you something. You know I've actually been working on that company for awhile now, trying to get them on board with us. You know, I've put in a lot of hours and what not, and it just kind of feels like you took them from underneath me. No hard feelings or anything, but I'm gonna talk to the big boss man this morning, and since I did a lot of the work to get them in the door and since you'll be managing the account, see if he agrees that we should split the commission on them. I think it's a pretty good deal for you. You know, I want you to get something for your role and all, and I don't mind taking a little less in order to help you out, you know?"

"Wait, what?"

"Uh, do I need to repeat all that?"

"I cold-called them a year ago, and have been keeping up with emails since then. What exactly have you done to 'bring them in' as you say?"

"Whoa, whoa, I can feel the tension rising in here, Lewis. There's really no reason to get upset for a misunderstanding and all. Besides just talk to John if you think that's not fair."

"I definitely will, but I'm asking you, James. What did you do to get this account?"

"I had a good bit of correspondence with Nancy through email, and was strategically moving them along."

"When did all this take place?"

"Well, it's no use arguing dates and specifics Lewis."

"It's actually really important that we figure this out, James. That commission is rightfully mine. I want to see copies of all your email correspondence to them on my desk by the end of today."

"What? I'm your boss, Lewis."

"Well, then act like one, and be willing to be accountable. Because right now it feels a lot like you're just a cheat, and I'm not going to be walked all over. I want the emails, James, and if you don't send them, I will tell John, all about this part of your recommendation to split the commission."

"Fine, let's just drop it ok. I don't need the extra bonus anyways. If it's that important to you, and if you're that greedy, then you can have it."

"Don't try and turn this into what it's not James. Oh, and by the way, Nancy is the lady that answers the phones. Bill is the owner. Did you ever talk to Bill?" I say, knowing I'll catch him with this one.

"Oh yeah, Bill and I are really close. I'm pretty sure we went golfing last year."

"I figured that," I say as I turn to my computer screen. Part of me wants to tell him that I just met with the owner, Luke, yesterday, but it's just not worth it.

For the rest of the day, I feel this agitation floating all around me. I try to avoid seeing him as much as is possible. I honestly just want to punch him. I feel like that would settle everything inside of me.

Later that day…

As I walk in the door from work, I'm greeted by Lily.

"Hi daddy," she says.

"Hey there princess, how was your day?"

"Pretty good. I made a new friend at school. She's new to the area and she loves to dissect animals in science class just like me."

"That's great honey. I'm so happy for you."

"Hey, where's your mom?" I say as I kiss her on the forehead.

"Oh I think she's in your bedroom."

"Ok, thanks honey. I'll see you later."

"Love you daddy."

"Love you too," I say as I smile back at her.

I drop my briefcase off on the chair and walk into our room. Sara is folding laundry on our bed.

"Hey there, salesman of the year," she says smiling.

"Today was not good."

"What do you mean? I thought they'd all be singing your praises."

I went on to tell her what happened with James.

"You're kidding me right," she says with her jaw dropped open. "Well, what do you think is going to happen?"

"I don't know Sara. I don't think he's going to press for splitting the commission anymore, but I don't trust him. I feel like he'll just try to do something else to mess with me."

"Oh, honey. I'm so sorry."

"Yeah me too."

"Well, why don't you go out and work on your chair till dinner is ready?"

"Yeah, that sounds good. Thanks, babe."

As I cut out the legs from some walnut wood my dad had left over, my mind replays the event of today. And then, in an instant, I can feel a physical peace wash over me. I turn and look toward the door to my shop. It's as if something or someone just walked through the door. My whole body feels like I just got dipped in peppermint essential oil. I know what that feels like because one time Sara gave me a back massage with straight peppermint oil. Not what I would call a relaxation technique.

I turn off the saw, walk over and sit down in the office chair and take a deep breath. And for the next five minutes, I bask in the warmth of what feels like an embrace from Heaven.

"Babe, dinner's ready," Sara yells from the house.

"I'll be right in," I respond. But really I just want to stay right here for as long as I can.

As I walk back to the house I notice the camp chair that was out in the middle of the yard folded up against the house. I laugh and think to myself, 'so now the kids decide to clean things up'.

After dinner we clean up and Sara and I talk about all that happened today.

"So, do you think you'll talk to James tomorrow about all of this again?"

"No, I don't even want to see James tomorrow."

"I'm sorry, this must feel awful for you."

"Yeah, I feel a little better after being out at the shop."

"So, I know that we've had some fun conversations about God's interaction with us. But I was wondering if you could tell me how you really feel about it," she says.

"Really? Why now?"

"I don't know Lewis. I guess I just want to be a part of your journey," she says.

"I don't really know what to think, Sara. It feels like I got to step into a new world for a moment and now I'm trying to figure out how it all works."

She puts the dishrag down and comes over and puts her hands on my face. "Please tell me about the other night. One thing I know about you Lewis is that you are trustworthy. And I trust you. I want to be a part of whatever you are walking through."

"Really?"

"Yes, really," she says with a chuckle.

"I just thought you were kind of mad at me for going through all of this."

"I uh, didn't see clearly at first. But I went and met with Pastor Tom and he helped me see a lot of stuff I couldn't. And that if you are walking into a season where you are growing, then it's gonna look messy to those around you. And the best thing I can do is encourage you to keep going. So, keep going," she says with a smile as she puts her arms around me and squeezes.

"Thank you," I say as tears start to fall from my eyes. "I don't know why that means so much, but it does."

"You're welcome babe."

I go on to tell her all about my experience the other night and all that Luke told me at our meeting. She sat there with wide eyes, and in that moment I could feel her heart saying, 'What if?'.

"Hey, I've got a new book that I'm really excited about, so I'm just going to read tonight. I'm fine if you want to work on the chair some more."

"Ok, thanks. I'll do that."

I lean down and kiss her and it feels like our first kiss. We both smile thinking that this mess is what it took to clear up the mundane life that had grown between us.

As I walk out to the shop I notice the camp chair set up in the middle of the yard. That's so strange. I didn't see the kids come outside after dinner at all.

Chapter 18

As I sit here shaping the spindles for the back of the chair, I begin to feel tired. I look down at my watch reading 11:00 pm. I should get to bed.

I walk toward the door and turn back to look at the finished pieces of wood that will soon be ready to put together. I feel accomplished, and excited. It's as if a part of me that I did not know existed has come alive. I turn out the lights and close the door.

As I turn to walk to the house, that voice inside of me turns my attention to the chair. I pause and think through getting up early for work, and the last time that I tried sitting down and it didn't work.

But something in me stirs and I decide to give it one more chance.

I put my hand on the back of the chair as I step up beside it, take a deep breath and sit down.

Here I am, I can't believe it. I'm back! The excitement pulsing throughout my whole body is exhilarating. I immediately begin to look around, realizing that I am at the same location as before on top of a mountain. Where is he?

Where is Ammoris? I don't see him anywhere. I stand up and begin to walk trying to see where I am. I can see the small pile of rocks up ahead that I noticed before and decide to go check it out.

As I approach this pile of rocks that someone clearly had to carry up to the top of this mountain, I chuckle. 'I'm glad it wasn't me'.

"Hello Friend," Ammoris says as he walks within view.

"Hi Ammoris," I say smiling excitedly. "I made it back. I tried to come back the other night, but something was wrong with the chair or something. I don't know, anyways, how are you doing?"

"Ha, Lewis, I love it when you come to visit. And thank you."

"Thank you for what?"

"Thank you for asking how I am. I can't remember the last time someone from your world asked me how I was doing," he said solemnly, but still maintaining his smile.

"Well, I just really like being around you, and I guess I just wanted to know," I say, not sure how to answer in this moment.

"Well, since you asked, I have felt sadness, much grief, however, I have a hope that allows all of those feelings to float instead of causing me to sink," he says with a chuckle.

"And how are you, my ancient friend?"

"Ancient friend? I don't know what that means, but I'm doing really good. You see I'm building a chair right now. I built one before, but it broke, and I got really angry. But I think I got really angry because of other stuff in my life, and I wasn't going to church. Oh yeah, Luke thinks you are actually Jesus. So I'm sorry about the church thing. I'm sure I'll go back, in fact just give me the order and I'm there."

"Slow down friend, while you are here with me you can truly be at peace. I know you are building a chair."

"How do you know that? Well, I guess if you know everything."

"I know because I put it in your father's heart to ask you to do that."

"Oh, I see."

"And Luke is a dear friend of mine. I was so excited for you to meet him the other day."

"Yeah, he really is a great guy."

"Oh yes, and as for you not being at church. I know about this as well," he looks at me with sadness as he pulls out a piece of paper from his cloak and unfolds it. "This attendance chart with your name on it, well Lewis, this is why I wanted to talk to you."

"Oh man, listen, I'm sorry. I thought I was doing the right thing I just wanted to figure stuff out, and I was so confused and…"

I stand there stammering as Ammoris starts laughing uncontrollably.

"Lewis," he says while still laughing. It's a list of songs I like, hahaha," he says as he turns the paper around to show me.

"Oh," I sigh deeply and shake my head.

"That was a good one. Oh man, I got you good on that one."

I pause and take a breath. "So, tell me which songs are your favorite ones Ammoris," I say a little annoyed but also laughing inside.

"Oh you've never heard them before."

"Try me. I like a lot of different types of music."

"No, I mean, these are songs that no one has heard except for me. They are the ones that some of my friends wrote for me and wouldn't play for anyone else. They are my favorites. They're like little treasures that I keep close."

"It doesn't seem like it's a very long list."

"No, it's not, but each song is priceless to me."

"Wow, that's pretty cool. Hey about church, are you really not mad at me about that?"

"Lewis, why do you think I would tell people to go to church?"

"I don't know, because you can learn more about You. Well, I mean, we can learn more about You."

"Nope, try again."

"I don't know, I'm the one currently not going."

"Lewis," he says with a chuckle. "It's the beauty and force of a group of followers whose hearts are longing to meet with me, that learn to follow me and to live in unity in this divided world. And then from there, they become a symbol, individually and corporately of the most powerful treasure on the earth. Love. If it's not that, then the reasons for it are simply human reasons and you won't find many people that are true to their hearts there."

"Huh, but don't you think people have good intentions even in their ignorance?"

"Lewis I always believe in the good intentions of people, but even the very best of intentions in the wrong direction will lead to the wrong endpoint. And if people are bent on the direction they think is right instead of waiting for and following the direction I am leading, then I'm afraid it's a sad ending."

"I see. So, is there anything you wanted to talk to me about?"

"Of course, there is a mountain of things I wanted to talk to you about, but the process of gaining understanding, wisdom, and connection to me is one that requires one step at a time, so I wanted us to meet up here again, this time. Do you remember being up here before the last time we met?"

"It's funny, it's like I have this feeling that I've been here before then, but I really don't remember it."

"Yes, I know. Lewis, if I told you that you and I have met here before, would you believe me?"

"Well, I don't remember it, so I don't know how to believe you, but I trust you."

"That's good enough for me," he says smiling. "Do you know what this pile of rocks is?"

"Yeah, I think so. It's called an altar, they used them in Bible times."

"Bible times," he says laughing. "You guys and your description of things."

"Why is that funny," I say.

"I don't know how to explain it, but trust me, there are a few things up here that we get a kick out of. Anyways, yes, it is an altar. This specific altar is actually yours. You've carried each one of those rocks up this mountain. You just didn't realize it."

"Uh, I think I'd have some sort of memory of that."

"Yes, you probably would. You see, I explained it another way to a young girl once. It's as if your life began on a mountain and then each painful circumstance brought you down into the valley. Your journey toward freedom was always about climbing back up the mountain, and once you made it to the top, the rock, or the circumstance that you overcame and found freedom in, was placed on this pile as an altar of remembrance. This, Lewis, is your life work, and I'm confident that this altar will be much larger as you continue your journey."

"Wow, so which one stands for what?"

"Go put your hand on one and find out."

As I walk hesitantly toward the pile I find one that is smooth all over. I look back at him to see him nodding at me. I place my hand on the rock and immediately a vision overtakes my mind. I can see my parents yelling and fighting. And then I see them years later embracing. Then the vision switches to me and Sara. I can see her heart and it looks like an ice block has encapsulated it. I'm standing in front of her as she is throwing darts at me. Each one hits my heart and burns deeply. In that moment I run to her embrace her and hold her tight. I can hear myself whispering to her that I love her and it will be ok. And then I see water pouring from her chest, revealing that the ice has melted.

I take my hand off of the rock and turn to Ammoris with tears in my eyes.

"Really? It makes that much of a difference?"

"Oh, son, if you only knew all that heaven rejoiced over. But freedom… Wow, I wish you could experience the party that goes on after one our sons or daughters gets true freedom. It's truly what I live for. Go ahead," he says as he motions for me to touch another rock.

I spend the next, however long it was, reliving memories of things I never thought were that big of a deal, and yet seemed huge to him.

"Ammoris?"

"Yes, Lewis."

"Why couldn't I come back the other night."

"You could've."

"What do you mean? I tried, I sat every which way in that chair."

"But did you respond when I called you?"

"You mean after I got up and was heading in the house?"

"Yes, Lewis. You see, our meetings are by invitation for now, once you finish your chair it will be different, but by then you will also be ready for the difference in our meetings."

"Oh, well I'm really close to being done, I can probably finish it in a couple of days."

"Hahaha, Lewis, you can always get me to laugh. I know you can, but what if you weren't supposed to. What if I asked you to wait until I made it clear that you were supposed to finish it?"

"But why? I mean I just want to be with you."

"I know you do Son, and I with you. But, life is not about who arrives at the finish line the quickest. It is about who has gained all the good gifts that they were supposed to, by the end of their race. And sometimes those good gifts take something your world knows very little about. I call it the 'art of waiting.'"

"By the sounds of it, I don't know if I'll like it."

"No, you may not be comfortable with it and you may not love every second of it, however, what you gain in it, is far more than you trying to receive anything without it. It's kind of like this. Let's say an angel came to you one day. He told you he had something for you and took you into the woods. You walked for a few miles until you arrived at a small clearing. There were two other large and armed angels that stood on either side of a chest. He opened the chest and showed you that it was full of gold and other treasures. It weighed 300 lbs. He said that you could either take it now or later. If you took it now, it would not be protected if you had to leave it somewhere, but if you left it where it was, it would stay safe until you came back to get it. What would you do? Oh yeah, one more thing, you have to carry it 3 miles back to your house."

"Oh man. That's heavy. I would probably just start dragging it as best as I could."

"Yes, of course. And why would you do that?"

"I'd be so excited about it. I figure even if I have to pay someone to help me get it back there, I'd still have more than enough for me."

"But either way, your determination and excitement would lead you to take a hold of it right away and start dragging. Am I correct?"

"Yeah, definitely."

"Would you think to ask the angel for any advice or help on getting it back?"

"Oh, well yeah, I probably would do that. I guess."

"Ok, so let's say that you ask him for advice and he hands you a paper that has a list of exercises that you must commit to doing for one year. Would you do that?"

"You mean and leave the gold there?"

"Precisely. Remember, it's already yours and it will stay safe."

"I don't know, that's a tough one."

"I know it is Lewis. And yet, so many people from your world are trying to drag around treasure chests that they have not been prepared to carry. And then, inevitably, they are giving up and leaving their gifts by the side of the road, simply because they did not understand the art of waiting. They became consumed with a treasure that they weren't even strong enough to carry. And this, my dear friend, is why you must listen to my leading. The chair that you are building will be perfect when it is built in the right timing, other than that it will just be a good chair. But, I really want you to build me a perfect chair. And I really want you to trust and come to understand my perspective of time and perfection."

"Ok."

"Lewis, there are more rocks that must be carried up here. Will you carry them?"

"I will Ammoris, I will."

"Thank you," he says with a smile as he approaches me and reaches out his arms to embrace me.

I bury my head into his chest and in that instant I find myself leaning forward in the camp chair in my back yard. As I sit there staring straight ahead at the trees that surround the perimeter of our yard, I realize I've never explored back there. With that thought, I stand up and walk back toward the house to find a rest that is truly peaceful and somewhat divine.

Chapter 19

3 months later...

"Hey honey, how was work today?" Sara says.

"Same old," I say as I hang up my coat on a hook by the door.

"Are you ok? You seem a little sad."

"Yeah, I guess I am a little sad," I reply taking a deep breath.

"Do you want to talk about it?"

"Maybe later, after the kids go to bed."

"Ok, sounds good."

"How was your day?" I say as I walk around the island in our kitchen and wrap my arms around her.

"It was really good. I had lunch with Meg, and we got talking about what if God spoke to us. Anyways, it was a very interesting conversation. Especially with all that you've been through."

"Well, what's her take on it all?"

"She just doesn't think it's possible, or that it matters. I tried to explain to her how it could deepen our relationship with God, but she just couldn't wrap her mind around it."

"You think it deepens our relationship with God? I thought you didn't think it happened either."

"You know Lewis, I've seen so much change in you in the last few months. It's like there is this grounding in you that wasn't there before. I can't help but believe that something is happening. I see the effects and honestly, I like them," she says as she looks into my eyes.

"Thanks, babe, that means more than you could know."

"So, dinner will be ready in about an hour. Did you want to go work on the chair for a little bit? I haven't seen you working on it for awhile. Did something happen?"

"Yeah, I've been working on some other projects. It's funny, the more I work on other things, the more I learn about the chair. I think I'm going to redo some of the parts that I was working on before. I mean, they were good before, but now I see how they could be better. But, I'm just not feeling led to get back to it, just yet."

"Got it, well, I know Mrs. Mayberry down the street keeps dropping hints about a squirrel oven rack puller."

"Haha, yeah, I'll get right on that," I say laughing.

"So, any word on James and work?"

"Just that I have a meeting with him and the owner next week. I mean, I know the guy doesn't like me. I just don't know if this is just a power trip, or if he really just wants me gone. I'm hoping that John can see through it."

"I can't believe you're going through all this. I'm so sorry. I'll be honest, I kind of want to go down there and tell him what I think about all of this. I mean, doesn't he have any sense of right and wrong?"

"I think he's just really lost, Sara. I think he is stuck in work being his life and identity, and he's consumed with being in control of it. Either way, I'm not worried about it. God has a plan for us."

"Yeah, I sure hope so," she says.

The next day…

My desk phone rings and I don't recognize the number.

"Hello?"

"Lewis! How are you doing friend?"

"I'm good, who is this?"

"Oh sorry man, this is Luke."

"Oh, hi Luke. Great to hear from you. How have you been?"

"Man, I'm doing great. Listen, I was on my walk this morning and the Lord told me to reach out to you. Any chance you have time for lunch?"

"Yeah, definitely. Where and when."

"How about Lockport's at 11:30am?"

"Sounds good. I'll see you there."

"Great, see you then."

The rest of the morning seems to drag. I review my accounts and make a few phone calls, but I'm relieved when it's time to leave for lunch.

"Hey man, good to see you," Luke says as he stands up from the table and gives me a hug.

"Good to see you too. So, what's the good word?"

"Oh yeah, we'll get to that. But first, have you had any more encounters? You know like the one you told me about?"

"Oh, yeah. Well, I did have one a few months back. It was pretty incredible. But not since then. He talked to me a lot about waiting on Him and the process for things taking time. I guess it helped me calm down a little bit and realize that just because things aren't visible right away, doesn't mean that they aren't happening."

"That's good, that's really good," he says nodding. "So, how are things at work going?"

"Pretty good I guess? I mean there seems to be some tension between me and my boss, but other than that, work is work."

"Got it, well. Because of my position, I can't go into details on all of this. But, I will tell you this. If you ever need a job, please just call me."

"Oh man, what is going on?" I say as a lump begins to form in my throat.

"Let's just say, your company probably isn't as loyal as you are. But listen, you are on a journey, and just because something is painful or feels bad, doesn't mean it's not supposed to be on your journey. Some of the most painful things I've experienced were strategically placed in my life in order to make me into something that I couldn't have become without them."

"Ok," I say wishing I could find out what he knows, but knowing that I'd be asking him to lay aside his integrity.

"So, how's your family doing?"

For the next hour, we swap stories about our lives and aspirations.

"So, what was it that God spoke to you about this morning on your walk?"

"Oh yeah, I don't know what this exactly means to you, but He said to tell you that you are about to carry your heaviest rock up the mountain and that as painful as it is, you'll make it. Any idea what that means?"

"Ha," I chuckle. "Yeah, I have a pretty good idea. Which can only mean that things are about to get interesting."

"Well, like I said before, if there's any way I can help you, please just let me know."

"Thanks, that means a lot."

"You got it. I got another meeting I gotta run to, but here's my cell number," he says as he hands me a business card. "Lewis, please feel free to give me a call anytime. You're not alone in this."

"I will, thanks."

As I walk back to the office I think about how it feels like I just received a warning for what's ahead, and yet have no way of knowing how to be prepared for whatever it is. It feels like I'm in this movie and everyone else knows what's going on except me.

Chapter 20

1 week later...

As I prepare as much as possible for this meeting with James and John, I'm reminded that I'm not alone in this one.

James stops by my office. "Hey, Lewis. John is ready for us."

He looks somewhat solemn. That's interesting. Maybe he's quitting and John is going to ask me to take over his position.

"Alright, I'll be right there."

As I walk into John's office, he greets me with a hello and a handshake. I've only spoken to him a handful of times throughout my time here. He was always cordial but not very welcoming.

I sit down and lean forward in my chair, waiting for what's to come. I look at both of them, to see who is going to explain why we're here.

"Well, Lewis, I guess I'll start," James says with a lack of confidence in his voice. "You see, there have been some concerns about you not being a team player, and causing some division in the office environment. You know it's really important that we stick together because a team is an unstoppable force."

What I want to say at this point is, 'nice slogan you read off of a website,' but I refrain.

He continues, "Lewis, we've always appreciated you working for us, but while others have been willing to put in the extra time, it seems that you've been leaving early."

"I'm sorry, can you explain early?" I interrupt.

"Oh well, you know it's more of a mindset that is different from the direction of the company."

"But in my agreement, it stated that I was in contract for 40 hours per week. Have I not done that?"

"You know it's not about specifics, it's more about the feeling that we are trying to be the best at what we do and honestly, some of the people around you feel like you don't really care about that or the company. And, it's probably better for you not to be tied to a place where you don't feel like you can give 110 percent. Do you understand?"

"I think I understand what is happening, but what's the bottom line, James?"

"Well, you know that's why we called this meeting…"

"Lewis," John interrupts. "Listen, I've always liked you. You're a family guy and an honest man. There is no doubt in any of that, and without you, that account we just got, may not have ever happened."

I turn and look at James who is rolling his eyes.

"John, please tell me that you have some amount of information about all of this 'negative behavior,' that has come from somewhere other than James. Can you do that, John? Because I'll be honest, he has never liked me, and when I sold the Faulkner account, he really started not liking me even more. Let me ask you this, John, if I leave who automatically takes over my accounts?"

"Well, they'll be dispersed among the other employees of course."

"Yes, who does the dispersing?"

"Well, James of course, that's his job."

"So, does James keep any of the accounts?"

"Well, if it's in the best nature of the company, then yes. However, not Faulkner of course, we already agreed that would be split up."

"What, why doesn't he want Faulkner now?"

"Listen, Lewis, let's stay on topic here," James interjects.

"That sounds great," I say as I sit back in my chair. "What's the bottom line?"

"Lewis, we're letting you go," James says smugly. "We're giving you one month's severance pay. You can pack up your things today. I'm sorry it didn't work out."

"Ok," I say as I stand and reach over the desk to shake John's hand. "Thank you for the work and severance." I turn and walk toward the door without looking at James. I don't feel embittered toward James, I just don't want the stain of his handshake and all that he stands for anywhere near me.

"Lewis," John says as I reach the door. "I'm sorry."

I turn to look at him. "I'm not."

I feel bad for John. He is the owner of a really successful company who is ruled by an employee who is ruled by greed. It doesn't feel like a place I should stay. But I am utterly confused as to why James isn't taking over Luke's account.

1 hour later…

This is the first time in years I've been home before lunchtime. I walk in the door and it's perfectly quiet. Sara and the kids won't be home for another few hours and I am not sure what to do with all the free time. I take off my tie and dress shirt, and feelings of being freed from a prison wash over me. I put on a pair of jeans, and a flannel and decide to work out in the shop. I make a sandwich and head out to the place where I've found so much peace in the last months of my life. As I walk to the shop I look over to where the camp chair sits in the middle of the yard. It's not there. There was a part of me that wanted to get away, but I guess not today. I remember the last time I sat in the chair, wondering what was back in the woods behind our property. I finish my sandwich and decide to go explore.

The first few yards are full of thick bushes and vines. Once I navigate my way through all of the obstacles it opens up a little bit to a forest full of evergreens. The branches all start at about ten feet off the ground and the floor of the forest is soft with pine needles that have fallen. It is beautiful and feels somewhat mystical. I continue to walk for at least a quarter of a mile, but the scenery doesn't change. And here I am in the middle of a forest I never knew existed right behind my house. I can hear songs that I've never heard before. The birds, and the movements of branches brushing against each other. A soft wind blowing through. It all feels like when I'm with Ammoris.

I sit down with my back against a tree and revel in the silence.

"Ammoris, thank you for this," I say. "Thanks for Sara and the kids, and for life."

I spend the next 5 minutes thanking him for everything that comes to mind.

"And thanks for getting me out of that job," I say knowing that in this moment I really am grateful for being free from that.

As I continue to sit here in the silence, the wind begins to blow through the forest and even though it should send a chill through my body, all I feel is the warmth of an embrace. And in this moment, I know I'm not alone.

That night…

"Hi honey," I say as I wrap my arms around her. "I'll finish the dishes, you go relax."

"Really?" She says as if I've never done the dishes before.

"Yeah, really. Do you want me to make you any tea?"

"Uh, maybe. What's up with you?"
"What do you mean?"

"You just seem different, lighter, and you're wearing a flannel."

"Yeah, I am. Do you like it?" I say turning from the sink toward her.

"Yeah, I like it," she smiles. "But I am trying to figure out what happened to my husband."

"We can talk once I get the dishes done. Go sit on the couch, and I'll be there in a minute."

"Ok, but I'm a little weirded out right now."

"Haha, honey, it's all good," I say laughing, knowing that it's about to be all not good.

As I hand her a cup of tea in her favorite mug and sit down next to her, I pat her leg and take a deep breath.

"So, how's the tea?"

"Good, the tea is fine, what's going on? Oh my," she stops and looks into my eyes. "Your meeting was today. What happened?"

"Well, I think it's probably going to be about perspective on this one."

"You lost your job. I can't believe it. What happened? Why would they do this? Did you explain all that you've done for them? I don't understand."

"Slow down, tornado."

Tornado is a term of endearment that I gave to Sara when more than three thoughts come out at the same time.

"Lewis, what are we going to do?"

"Listen, I know there's a lot of feelings with this right now."

"A lot of feelings? These are realities, Lewis. We can't pay our bills on my income alone, and we're going to have to put Sammy and Lily in public school, and the list goes on.

"Hey listen, they gave me a month of severance pay."

"Well, whoopdy do da. We got a month of pay." She exclaims while whirling her finger in the air.

"Whoopdy do da? Sara come on," I say chuckling.

"No, Lewis you come on, this is a big deal and I don't have a clue how you are so nonchalant about it. Please tell me how this isn't a big deal to you?"

"Because I sat in the woods this afternoon," I say sheepishly.

"What? Are you crazy? Because you sat in the woods, now everything is going to be ok? Lewis, I need some time and space to process all this. But I will tell you this. You better start finding a solution right away because a month is going to go by really quick. And I don't know what our conversation at the end of the month is going to look like if you haven't found a way to do your job and support this family."

"Ok honey. I'm gonna go to the shop and work for a little bit."

"Fine."

I stop before I leave the room and turn to her. "Sara, I love you."

She puts her head down into her hand as she reaches with the other for the box of tissues.

I turn on the lights to the shop and walk to the work table. I put down my cup of coffee and run my hand across the smooth yet worn table. I look at all the measurements that are written all over the top. Years of my dad's work laid out on the wood in mathematical equations. Dents and chips cover the surface, the edges having all been softened. And then my hand stops in the middle of the table and my eyes squint to focus on words that have been etched into the wood. 'It's time'. Is all it reads. I look to the side of the table and see the book from my dad opened to the chapter on building a chair.

I smile and know deep down within that it is time to move forward. I pull out the pieces that for months have been stored away with a purpose and perfect timing shaped into each one.

I begin to notch the legs where they will fit together and then sand, until I think I'm done sanding, and then sand some more. As I glue the pieces and begin fitting them together, there's an excitement that comes over me. It's finally happening. I can see it start to take shape. I glue and place the legs into the holes on the bottom of the seat and then turn it right side up.

I take a step back and look at it. Wow. Who would've thought that I would enjoy this? I think. I walk over and sit down in the office chair, put my hands behind my head and lean back. I look over at the clock on the wall.

"Whoa it's late. I should get to bed."

I just need to build the back rest of the chair and stain it and I'm all done.

Chapter 21

For the first time in a long time, Sara and the kids are gone before I wake up. It feels strange to wake up and not get ready for work on a weekday. Part of me feels a little bit of guilt, like maybe I should be doing more. But, the other part of me is loving this break.

Somewhere around 8 a.m. I decide to get up and make some breakfast. As I pour myself some coffee, I look around and think about the fact that usually, I am rushing around here in the morning, then grabbing whatever is quick and running out the door. I take a deep breath and think about what I would enjoy eating. I grab the cutting board from the drying rack next to the sink and look out the window toward our backyard.

Excitement leaps inside of me as I see the chair set up in the middle of the yard. I forget about breakfast, grab a sweatshirt and my coffee and head outside. As I approach the chair I take one more sip of coffee and set it on the ground. I sit down confidently.

Immediately I find myself sitting on a rock ledge very high up the side of a mountain.

"WHOAA!!!" I yell as I scoot back as far as I can. As soon as my brain catches up with what my eyes are perceiving I feel suddenly not as confident as before I sat down. I try to take a deep breath as I sit here, but I can't seem to get any amount of oxygen in. Just then I hear him off to my right.

"Lewis, how are you, my friend?"

"Uh, I've been better," I say as my voice trembles.

"Lewis are you scared of heights?"

"More like terrified," I say still looking out in front of me.

"Oh my, then why are you so close to the edge?" He says laughing.

"Very funny, how do I get off of here?"

"Well, there are a couple of ways, but which would you prefer?"

"Um, the one that keeps me alive and not falling, and is really quick," I respond through short and quick breaths.

"Hahaha Lewis, even when you're scared you are still really funny. I love that about you," he says as he walks across a very narrow path toward me. "Here, let me help you up."

"Ok, yeah, that's good," I say as I take his hands and allow him to pull me to my feet. "Where do we go now?"

"Before we go anywhere you've gotta calm down, you'll get yourself killed out here like that."

"Ok, how do I do that?" I say still holding onto all the panic as I gaze out over the expanse that falls suddenly past my feet.

"Well for starters, stop looking at all the things that are making you like that."

"Oh yeah, ok, that's good," I say short of breath.

"Now Lewis, look at me."

As my eyes meet his, I'm met with a confidence unlike anything I've experienced before. I finally am able to take a deep breath that comes out so naturally. I feel the wind blowing against me and it feels refreshing instead of terrifying. It is as if he is more stable than even the mountain under my feet. With my hands in his and my eyes locked on him, fear vanishes.

"Now follow me, Lewis," he says as he turns and walks on the narrow path that he came from.

We walk for a little while when I realize I'm carrying a backpack that feels pretty heavy. The trail finally opens up and gives us more breathing room than before. He stops until I am beside him and then we continue walking side by side.

"Where are we Ammoris?"

"We are on our way to your freedom."

"Huh?"

"Do you remember the altar? And how I told you that you had brought the rocks up there?"

"Yeah, I remember."

"Well, you are in the middle of one the harder climbs you've done to this point. And I knew you'd need some direction with what's ahead."

"Ok, well things seems to be going pretty good back home. I mean, I've got a month of pay till I really need to get back to work, and Luke said I could work for him. So, I'm thinking it should all be pretty easy."

"I know it looks that way. But your journey isn't just about all the pieces fitting nicely together. It's also about the changes that your heart needs to make, and that can be the most painful part of any journey."

"So, what changes will my heart need to make?"

"Lewis, even if I told you, it still wouldn't change the need for the process. It's an antsy world that you exist in. It seeks to avoid process at all cost. 'Just get me to the ending', they all say, but they miss out on experiencing anything of substance or true value. I just need you to know that as painful as this part of your journey is, it is full of purpose. And you may not understand this, but please don't work for Luke. That isn't the path I've laid out for you."

"Really? But I thought he was a good guy, and one of your friends."

"More than you know. I love Luke. But 'good' does not always equate with my plan. And you cannot always know my plan from asking everyone around you what they think or sense, even if they are close to me," he said as he patted my head like a father who is proud of his son. "Now that we are communicating, their voices will either confirm what I am saying, or lead you in a different direction, but ultimately it's up to you to decide which way you will go. My path will always lead you to the true blessing, while any other path will lead you in circles, or back down the mountain. You have to be on guard from counterfeits, they will feel and look so right, but they will always lead you away from me."

"I don't want that Ammoris, not at all."

"I know you don't Lewis, but some of the tests that you will need to walk through are so difficult and painful. You will feel like you are dying in order to follow me, but even that is on purpose, because there are parts of you, things that you've picked up throughout your life, that must die in order for you to be able to continue to walk with me."

"Ok," I say waiting for him to explain more.

He stops and turns to me and smiles.

"You see that," he says as he points up ahead.

I look and see a peak in the far distance. It looks like it would take days to get there.

"Yeah, it's really far."

"And treacherous," he says smiling.

"And what about it," I say hoping that he is going to give me another analogy of life, instead of telling me that's where we are headed.

"Well, that's where we're headed."

"Yep, I kind of figured. What about this back pack. This thing is pretty heavy."

"I know. This one has some weight to it because, well, it's one of the hardest ones to find freedom from."

"Well what is it?"

"It's provision."

"I don't understand, I thought the things I carried to the altar were things that I was supposed to heal from and find freedom from."

"Yes, that is true, but this provision is actually the deception. It tempts you to believe that your provision comes solely from you and your work."

"But doesn't it?"

"It does if you would like it to. You see most people love to choose their own paths. They try and bolster themselves up so that they will feel like they are the value in life. However, when they get to the end of their life they all have the same thoughts pass through their mind. 'Who was I? Why was I really here? Did I really do anything of worth?' You know, I've seen people do incredibly good things on this earth, come to the end and ask those same questions. Simply because they weren't connected to the source of who they are. And if you're not doing good things from a place of being connected to where you truly came from, then you won't be able to see the good work as anything that fills you up, because it simply won't. And so it is essential that you understand provision from my perspective. It is not just my promise to you to provide for your needs. It is my joy. But, if you have expectations on how much and when and what my provision should look like, then it is inevitable that you will be disappointed. And so with everyone, there must be a process of purging from the mindset of what you deserve. It is not easy or comfortable, but it is necessary. My dear friend, Lewis, if you are going to follow me, then you must understand all of this and choose to see life differently from those around you."

"Ok Ammoris. Well, how long will it take us to get there?"

"That my friend, will be left up to time. But I will tell you this. The quickest way there, is through surrender and obedience. That's also the way that you'll get the most out of it."

"Got it. Are you going to be with me the whole way there?"

"Of course I will be, Lewis. I'll be right here beside you. But you might not feel like I'm beside you down there. And that's ok if you can't feel me there. It just means you will have to rely on what you know is true of me here. Do you understand?"

"Yes I do."

"Lewis it's going to be a great adventure," he says smiling, but then looks seriously into my eyes. "But don't forget, adventures have really great parts, and really painful parts. Don't change who I know you are because of pain."

"Thank you Ammoris, I will try not to."

With that he puts his hand on my shoulder and everything fades into a white light that becomes the sun shining down on my face as I sit up in the camp chair in the middle of my back yard. I take a deep breath and reach down for my coffee.

"Still hot," I say out loud. "How does that even work?"

I spend the rest of my day in the shop working on the backrest for my chair. Each piece crafted as if time doesn't exist and each tick of the clock has no weight on the worth of my task.

Chapter 22

5 days later...

I can faintly feel the buzzing in my pocket from my cell phone. I turn off the sander I am using and put it on the work bench.

As I pull my phone out of my pocket. I can see it's Luke calling. Immediately the memory of Ammoris telling me not to work for him comes back to my mind.

"Hey man, how's it going?"

"It's going good Lewis. Hey, I just heard the news from James that you weren't with them anymore. Are you doing ok?"

"Yeah, I'm doing really good. Just enjoying the break."

"Good, that's good. Listen, I'm calling to tell you I meant what I said. I've got a position here, and I think you'd be perfect for it, I just have one thing I wanted to talk about. I just don't think it would be fair if..."

"Luke," I interrupt as nice as possible. "Listen, I can't, I mean, I don't think I'm supposed to come work for you."

"Really? Do you have another offer?"

"No, I don't."

"But I don't understand. I mean, are you guys going to be ok financially?"

"Yeah, for now we will. Listen, if it were up to me, I'd love to come work with you. I think it would be so much fun, I just know that I'd be doing it because it was a good thing, but not necessarily a God thing. Does that make sense?"

"Haha, more than you know, friend. Well, listen, let's get lunch sometime soon. Shoot me a message with what works for you."

"That would be really great."

"Oh and Lewis, the value of obedience is not measured here on earth, but where it is measured, it's like diamonds."

"Thanks, Luke," I chuckle. "Talk to you later."

"Same."

Later that day…

"Hi honey, how was your day?" I say as Sara walks in the door.

She drops her things on the island and sits down on a stool.

"It was tough," she says as she sighs.

"I'm sorry, what happened?"

"It just, I don't know. I am one of the few people there who actually desires things to be better and wants good change to happen, and yet it seems like all I face is resistance. I just wish I had it as easy as you right now."

"Yeah, I'm so sorry. Is there anything I can get for you?"

"No, I just need a break."

"Well, I'll make some soup for dinner. Why don't you go get in the tub and relax for a little."

"Really?"

"Yeah, of course."

"Ok, thanks."

As I stand here at the island chopping up vegetables, Sammy and Lily come bounding in the door.

"Hey guys, how was school today?"

"Pretty good," says Lily.

"Yeah it was fine," adds Sammy.

"Well, what do you guys say about heading out to the park once I get dinner started?"

"Yeah, that would be great dad," they reply.

"Alright, go ahead and get started on homework and then we'll head out in about thirty minutes."

They take off down the hall to their rooms and I continue chopping.

I wonder what that comment was from Sara. I mean is she really mad at me that I get a break? Or is she mad about me not looking for work?

After we get back from the park, we sit down and warm up with a nice bowl of dad's specialty. Chicken noodle soup. I wouldn't consider myself a chef, but I do love to cook soup. And this one is my favorite. Simple, yet so heart warming at the same time.

After dinner Sara and I work on cleaning up together. As we stand side by side at the kitchen sink, I look over at her as she stares out the window. Her stare is heavy as if there is a huge weight that is wrapped around her mind.

"So, anything you want to talk about?" I say, prying just a little bit, because if there is a lake full of emotions I don't want to break the dam, just help some of the water over the spillway.

"Hmm," she pauses. "No, I don't think so."

"Ok, that's fine."

"Really? It's fine?"

"Well, yes, if you don't want to talk about anything, than I'm not going to force you."

"I just don't understand how you can't see it?" She responds with excitement growing in her tone.

"Can you give me a word picture to help me?" I say trying not to laugh, but really wanting to ease into these murky waters.

"Ughh, Lewis. You just don't get it."

"But that's what you're here for honey. I need your help to get it," I say still holding back my laughter, but unable to conceal the smile.

She looks over at me with a look that says, 'this is not a laughing matter'.

"Listen honey. I'm sorry if you're angry, but I need help understanding what's making you angry."

"Fine, I'll spell it out for you. You don't have a job," she says articulating each word. "My job won't pay for everything we need. We won't make it if you don't do something, and on top of that you don't seem to care about any of it."

"Well, I did have a job offer today, but I didn't take it."

"What?" She exclaims. "Are you kidding me? I don't care if it was McDonald's calling, you need to reconsider your priorities. Staying home and slacking off isn't an option, and it isn't the Lewis I married."

"No, it was actually much better than McDonald's," I say hesitantly.

"What was it? Can you still accept it?"

"No, I can't. It was with Luke's company, the guy that we sold that big account to before I was let go."

"Wait, you what? You mean to tell me that you lose your job and then God brings along another better job, with a guy that you told me loves God, and you turn it down. Ohhh, this getting really rich. I can't believe you Lewis. I honestly can't believe this is happening. The ship is sinking, and you are sitting there sipping tea."

"Babe, you know I don't really drink tea," I throw out as a last-ditch effort to calm the situation in some way.

"Ahhh, Lewis, not now, not your jokes, this is serious," she says placing her hands down on the edge of the sink and hanging her head.

"Ok, I'm sorry. Listen, Let's go sit outside and talk. I'll tell you what's going on and maybe that will help you to see where I'm coming from."

"Fine, but I don't think it will help our reality."

"Maybe not. I'm going to make myself a cup of coffee, do you want some? Or I could make you some tea," I say with a smile.

She glares at me as she puts the last plate in the drying rack and walks out back onto the deck and sits down.

I walk out with two cups of coffee and hand her one.

"A peace offering for my lady," I say as I hand her the cup.

"Try a diamond necklace," she says half smiling, but still holding on to her anger and frustration.

"Maybe someday I will, if I can ever get a job, that is."

"Lewis, aren't you afraid at all?"

"I should be, I mean, before all of these times with Ammoris, I would've been. But somehow even though I have these moments of worry that try and overtake me, I just know that this is a part of the process."

I go on to share with her all about my last time with Ammoris and all that he told me about this part of our season and how it was necessary. I also told her about what he told me about Luke and how I wasn't supposed to work for him. As I finish, I look over at her, waiting for a response.

"Ok, well I just really hope this is all real. I mean, this is kind of out there, that you are talking to God and all, and it's just hard for me to trust it, you know."

"I know it must be hard. I can't imagine what it would be like to be on the other side of all this. Thank you for not giving up on me."

"Well, I haven't completely ruled out giving up on you, so don't get too comfortable," she says as a smile forms on her lips.

"I'll remember that," I say as I reach over and take hold of her hand.

Chapter 23

3 weeks later...

The pressure is starting to become unbearable. I received my last severance check a week ago, and haven't heard anything from anywhere on a new job. I'm half tempted to call Luke and ask him, but that would probably be awkward, and I don't know if he'd go for it.

The camp chair hasn't been left out for me and I have no clue what Ammoris is up to. I just wish I could have some sort of confirmation that this is really the right way to go.

Honestly, I was doing really good until the day after my last check. And then all of a sudden it hit me. The rope has been cut and I'm hanging on the side of this cliff, not sure if I can climb any further, and feeling like at any moment I'll lose my grip and start falling. I try to remind myself that I just need to trust, but I don't even know what that means, or what exactly I'm supposed to trust in. Am I trusting for a new job? Or am I trusting for a check in the mail from some stranger? I feel lost and in many ways desperate. I check my email about every half hour, run to the mailbox each day and have become obsessed with this idea that a message from someone who holds the answer is what I'm waiting for. Why am I waiting so long for this?

I roll out of bed and get dressed. I pour a cup of coffee and head out to the shop. I decide to listen to our pastor's sermon from last week. He is talking about trust, how convenient. I chuckle as I listen while working on the chair. He goes on to talk about how we tend to trust in the ways of God. 'You cannot trust in God doing this or that thing. Because we are not the master craftsman. Instead you must solely and decidedly trust in Him alone'. He says with conviction.

I set the stain and rag that I was using on the chair, down and decide to walk outside.

"God, I'm sorry," I say as I take a deep breath exhaling all of the worry and anxiety that has hovered over me this past week. "Please help me to trust, when I cannot see a way."

I'm reminded of my talks with Ammoris, and how he is always able to answer my questions at their root. It's like he somehow ignores my words and speaks to my heart cry instead.

"Ok," I say as I face the back woods. "I'll follow you, wherever you lead."

And in that moment a peace washes over me and a slight breeze brushes past my senses. And here in this place of surrender, I know that all will be ok.

I'm jolted out of this divine moment by my phone ringing in the shop. I walk in and pick it up.

"Hi Luke, so good to hear from you man. How are you doing?"

"Great Lewis, did you hear the news?"

"Uh, no I didn't"

"You're not gonna believe this, we just got an account with one of the biggest firms on the East Coast."

"Wow, that's great Luke, I'm so excited for you."

"Excited for me? How about for you?"

"What do you mean?"

"Lewis," he says with a chuckle. "Did you read the contract that I sent back over with the addendums?"

"Uh, yeah I think so?"

"No you didn't."

"Ok, no I didn't, I'm sorry I just figured it wasn't that different from the original, so I just handed it over to John to sign."

"This is crazy, I can't believe you never knew about this. Anyway listen, in the contract I put that your commission on this account was irrevocable even if you left the company. I called the owner to make sure that he understood that, so according to my figures, your commission just went from $500 a month to $5000 a month."

"Wait, what? Really?"

"Oh yeah, haha, and you don't even have to go to work for it. God is so good, isn't he? I mean you know what's really funny. When I called you a few weeks ago about working for us, I was about to tell you that I didn't think it would be fair for you to be still getting that commission from your old company and then working for us as well, and so I was going to ask if you'd be willing to release that, but you cut me off before I even got to it. Just think of that, if you would've ignored what God said about not working for me, you would've missed out."

"Wow, I'm still really stunned."

"I bet, well I hope that the commission is enough for you guys to make it through this season, however long it is."

"It really is, I can't believe it. Thank you for doing that and writing that into the contract, but how did you know all this was going to happen?"

"Hahaha, I didn't. I was just following orders."

"Ha, yeah. I get it."

"Hey how about lunch tomorrow, to celebrate."

"That sounds great, just let me know when and where, and I'll see you then."

I hang up the phone and look out the side window of the shop to see the camp chair sitting there.

Overtaken with excitement I run to the chair and plop down. The intense rush of entering another reality feels just as shocking to my system as it did before. I wake up and am at the same place I first met him, at the top of the mountain. I look around and see the altar. I walk over to it and as I brush my hand across the large stone on top I watch a screen that displays my struggle over the last few weeks.

"There he is," I hear from behind me.

I turn around to see Ammoris walking toward me.

"I wasn't sure if you were going to make it up here," he chuckles.

"Really?"

"I'm just joking, I knew you'd make it on this one. Now the next one I'm not so sure about, but we'll see," he says smiling.

"Nice, well I'll give it my best shot whatever it is."

"I know you will. You know Lewis, when you can see your life from up here, you are able to process pain in a way that doesn't leave you debilitated. But if you're perspective is only from life down there, then the situations you go through will rule you and move you all over the place. But that is why we are on this journey, is it not?" He says with a big smile. "So, I hear you've got some exciting news."

"Yeah, I figured you'd know about it. I can't believe it. Thank you."

"You're welcome," he says with the sincerity and gentleness of a generous father.

"How is it that you can organize and put all of this together, when there are so many things going on in the world, and it feels like time moves so fast."

"Ahh yes, there is the key. For you time moves fast, but here time does not exist. By the way, how was your coffee that was still hot after our last meeting?" He says laughing.

"It was very good," I chuckle. "I'm not sure how to wrap my head around that though."

"You can't. Your head will never wrap around it. But the more, 'time'" he says making quotation marks with his fingers, "you spend up here, the more you'll begin to understand."

"Sounds good. I would love to spend more time up here, it's just that I can only seem to get here when the chair is out."

"Well, have you finished the chair you were supposed to build yet?"

"Yeah, I just have some small touch-ups on the stain and then I have to seal it."

"That's wonderful Lewis. I'm so proud of you, and I know someone else who will be very proud of you also."

"Dad?" I say quietly.

"Yes Lewis, your father has been cheering you on since you began."

"Can I see him?"

"I wish that you could, but it's just not the right time."

"Well, when would it be the right time?" I say prying a little bit.

"Lewis, the secrets of my existence are extended to you as I see fit. They are not in some box that at some point you get access to and can take whatever you would like from. That kind of mindset will be a person's downfall. You see the temptation is always rooted in, 'if you do this, you'll be like me'. The temptation is to get you to grasp for things that are not yours to hold onto, instead of trusting my leading and waiting on me to give you what I know that you can hold. You see, I invite you into friendship, but you must never equate our friendship with equality. I am who I am and you are my masterpiece, which if you ask me, is a very important title. However, a masterpiece is not greater or equal to the master who created it. And so it must be this way."

"Yes master," pours off my lips in sincerity and understanding as a smile forms across my face revealing a divine piece of knowledge that was received and understood. And in this moment there is no shame in recognizing my place, no longing to be somewhere further in our relationship. There is simply confidence in that I am right where I am supposed to be.

"Come here Lewis," he says as he motions me to walk over to his side.

As I walk over to him, he holds out his arm and puts it around my shoulder and pulls me in close.

"That Lewis, is a good altar of freedom, but if you keep following me, it will be so much bigger."

"How is that possible? I mean, I don't have any like major hidden sin in my life."

"It is possible because your perspective of sin is incomplete. You've been taught that sin is a tangible action that someone at some point deemed wrong. But my definition of sin is anything that causes any amount of division between us. Sin, in essence, can only be perceived by the separation it creates. And although in following me, you've been given the opportunity to be free from all of it, it is the journey up this mountain that you must take each time, that allows you to truly be free. Freedom starts in your mind, but if it isn't walked out, then it is not complete. Many people down there tout their freedom, from a prayer they prayed. They believe that at the beginning of their journey they receive everything they will ever need. And the path that they think gets them there, is simply saying it over and over again. Think about it this way. It is as if when a person decides to follow me, they receive a shopping list. On the list is all of the things that are possible, but they still need to travel to the location where that item exists and pick it up, put it in their cart and pay for it, whatever the cost. And that doesn't happen as easy as just driving to the grocery store. It looks more like these trips that you've made up this mountain. Do you understand?" He says as he looks over at me.

"I do. So, I'm kind of just along for the ride?"

"That is the other perspective, Lewis. You are either driving and in charge or along for the ride. At least those are the only two human perspectives that one could come to the conclusion of. But the way it truly is, is that you are with me on the journey, and it is your journey to freedom. I'm the only one that knows the way and so you must trust me and follow me to get to where you need to be. Yes, I will drive, but you must engage in the journey and be active in it. I'm not interested in dragging people across the finish line," he says laughing.

"I think I understand."

"I know you do, son."

"Hey Ammoris, can you help me with Sara? I mean, I want her to understand all of this, but it just seems like as much as she wants to try and understand, she still has this wall up that I can't seem to do anything about."

"I know she does. But Lewis, that wall is not about you. It is about me. And yes I am doing something in Sara's life, but it is different than your journey. You will need to trust the process and be a sounding board for her. Stay gentle with her heart and questions and frustrations. And when it is appropriate, point her to me. Is there anything else on your mind?"

"No, I don't think so."

"Ok, friend. The next time you would like to meet with me, use your chair!" He says with a smile.

"Ok," I chuckle. "I will."

"Oh yes, and Lewis, there is one more thing that is essential for you to know. If you ever feel like you can't understand my way, I left a guidebook down there for you. Well, to be honest I like to think of it more as a love story, but you'll understand once you read it."

"That's great. How do I find it?"

"Well, it just so happens to be the book with the most sales ever recorded, which is humorous with how many times they've tried to get rid of it. It's funny to me how the smallest of people can try and make themselves appear so large and in control, and yet the only thing that fills them up to feeling large is all in their mind. Anyways, that's beside the point. Goodbye, Lewis," he says with a look of divine friendship and sincerity written across his face.

And the light dims, bringing my awareness back to closed eyelids and a calm afternoon sitting in my backyard.

Chapter 24

3 days later...

The polyurethane is finally dry on the chair. I stand at the door of the shop looking at this beautiful creation that feels like it took way too long to complete. I can't wait till Sara gets home so that I can show it to her.

The thought passes through my mind of Ammoris telling me to use this chair the next time I come to see him, so I decide to give it a try.

I pick it up off the workbench and carefully carry it outside to the middle of the yard. I set it down and smile. I look up at the woods behind our fence and remember my time talking to Ammoris while I was back there. I ponder the difference between when I was back there and when I've met him on the mountain. On the mountain our conversations would be very profound and he would give me such clear direction, but in the woods, this peace seemed to envelop me and his answers just seemed to well up from inside of me. The two seemed on different planes, yet so very similar in their outcomes.

With a hint of hesitance, I sit down in my hand crafted chair. I take a deep breath and the sensations I am waiting to experience, simply do not come.

Somewhat confused I move around a little bit, but still nothing.

Was it a trick? How am I supposed to understand what to do next if this isn't going to work? I stand up somewhat frustrated and walk toward the back of our yard. I stare through the brush and trees lining our property and shake my head.

"All I want, Ammoris, is to be where you are. I find such peace there, I'm so happy when I'm with you. Nothing seems impossible and I don't feel heavy like I do here. I'm sorry if I did something wrong that kept me from being able to get back to you."

I turn and walk back toward the chair. As I reach to pick it up, the moment my hand touches the back of the chair, a sensation pulses through my body. I pull my hand back quickly reacting to what was unexpected. I slowly sit down and the sensation returns, all around me I feel as if I have been dunked in ice-cold water, but I haven't lost my breath, at least not yet. I sit there and take in the sensations as a whisper like a breeze passes through me.

It whispers, "Lewis, I am here."

"Ammoris," I say while beginning to cry from the intense sensations enveloping my nervous system.

"Lewis, you must learn a new way to be with me, it will sustain you through your time here." Again it comes like a whisper in the wind.

"But can I ever come back there, to be with you?"

"You are just as much with me now as you were then. But it is not for you to decide or determine coming back to the mountain."

"Yes, master," I say smiling. And in that moment I can feel his smile like a wave of heat that is enveloping me.

"Thank you for remembering, Lewis, but don't ever forget, that as much as I am Master, I am also that much father, mother, and friend."

And the wind stops and instead of intense emotions, every cell of my body feels complete peace. It's the kind of peace that makes you feel like you could stop breathing and still be alive.

"I won't forget, Ammoris. I won't forget," I whisper.

Chapter 25

40 years later...

"How do we sum up a man's life? My father spent the first half of his life trying to find purpose and the last half living it out. He went from following what everyone else thought was the right way, to being consumed by the only direction that really ever mattered to him, which was following his best friend, Jesus. I can't list out all the accomplishments that my dad had on this earth, and honestly, most of them wouldn't be valued for what their true worth was. However, I can tell you this last week, he entered into his true home with a smile on his face and a heart full of life. He would always tell me that I would only ever be satisfied when I found the One who created me. And he was right. After years of struggling through life, I finally took his advice and can confidently say that I met the one who changed my dad."

"He would love nothing more than to know that on this day of celebrating his passing into eternity, we shared his life's message with everyone here. He wasn't a preacher or even a deacon. He didn't go to Bible College or have the knowledge of scholars. But he did have this…" and with that Sam walked off the stage and came back carrying a wooden chair that was worn from years of use.

"He had an access point to meeting with God. It truly is an incredible story. I remember asking him plenty of times about it, but the most recent time he told me something I didn't remember him ever telling me before. He told me that not long after using this chair to sit with and talk with God, that God had allowed him a memory that was of before he was ever born. He said it was like a very quick flashback, but after that he understood something about our lives on this earth that he had never been able to grasp before that time."

"That simple interaction and memory caused him to see all of life differently. He then knew without a doubt that this wasn't his true home. And what's funny is that most people would think this would cause you to become disconnected from your family and life here, but I can attest to the fact that for my dad, it caused him to live so full of vibrance, life and love. He was never the same. His care for me and my sister and mom were," Sam stops as tears begin to well up in his eyes. "I'm sorry. His care for us was divine."

"You all know how difficult it was for us at the end. With him not being able to walk and his communication deteriorating it was painful to watch. But I'd like to share one last story with you of the end of his time here."

"I was getting ready to leave mom and dad's house to go home for the evening. I had tucked dad into bed and kissed him on the forehead. He reached up and grabbed my arm and pulled me close. He whispered more clearly than I had heard him speak in months. He said, 'Son, tell them to build a chair, they must build a chair,' these words, poured across his lips as tears began to well up in his eyes. I responded 'I will Dad, I will.' That was the last time I saw my father alive on this earth."

"I returned the next morning to take care of him and when I arrived he had passed. In the corner of the room was this chair and a small table. My dad had not been able to walk or even crawl for the past few months. But when I walked into that room, he was sitting in the chair with his head resting on his open, worn out Bible. It wasn't until I picked him up to carry him back to the bed that I realized he was gone, and as I laid him on the bed, I looked up at his face to see that he was still smiling. As I walked back over to the table to look at his Bible, I saw that it was opened to John 15:15. There was a highlighter on the table next to his bible that was missing its cap, and there were two words that had been highlighted in the verse, 'servants' and 'friends'."

"Friends, family, he wanted you to know that this chair symbolized a relationship and a friendship that is of the utmost importance. But, I also believe he wanted us to know that the pathway to friendship with God always begins with understanding and submitting to being a servant."

"He is still smiling right now and believes in each one of you and the purpose of your journey while here on this earth. You see, before the tick of the clock of my dad's life, he existed. And after the last tick of his life he still exists. But what was here in between was the opportunity. Don't waste your opportunity. Build a chair, and find your true home!" Sam says as he walks off the stage and sits down next to Sara.

Sara leans over and kisses him on the cheek.

"He would be saying, 'thank you', right now," she says with tears in her eyes.

"Thanks Mom," Sam replies.

The line of attendees was long and it seemed as if each one had their own story of how Lewis had impacted their lives. Some stories were from situations where he had helped them or given them something they needed. Some were from his ability to simply sit and listen and encourage with what appeared to be divine wisdom. But all of them had this in common, he never received the glory, in every circumstance he would always share what Jesus had done for him and that he was merely a servant to the most generous king and friend a guy could ever know.

<u>Epilogue</u>

"Ammoris!" I whisper, as the light reaches my eyelids and convinces them to open.

I look up to see his hand reaching down waiting for me to take it.

I smile as I reach up and feel his warmth in my hand and immediately throughout my being.

"How are you friend?"

"Wow, that was indescribable."

"Haha, yes, that is a good way of putting it."

I look down at my hands and recognize the wrinkles are all gone. I run my hands across my face, and its smooth sharp features cause me to shake my head in amazement.

"Remember the coffee?" He asks while chuckling.

"Haha, yes I do. I also remember the stones from before."

"I know, it is possible now for you to carry all of the memories. Tell me Alois, what was your favorite of the stones?"

"They were all so amazing, but it had to be love, but not just love, it was the second side of it."

"What do you mean, Alois?"

"The obedience, and the surrender… When I found that place and then experienced the love that dwells there, it was incomprehensible."

Ammoris smiles at me with true joy.

"You found home, Alois, at least a very essential part of it. And you found what makes me who I am," he says as he puts his arm around me. "There's something I want you to see."

"Ok," I say as we begin to walk.

As we approach a huge mound of rocks he turns to me smiling.

"This is the reward, Alois, your freedom symbolized right here, and your treasure, well… I need to show you one more place," he says as we begin walking down a path that is leading us down the mountain.

What would normally take someone hours and hours seems to take us just the perfect amount of time needed for our conversations.

As we arrive at a beautiful stone wall that appears to have been here for very long, I see an ornate metal gate just up ahead.

"Go on," he says, motioning me to go through the gate.

As I open the gate and walk through, waves of intense pleasure and joy overtake me. I stop and look back at him, waiting for an explanation. Instead, he just stands there smiling. I begin to walk through this garden that is beyond what words can describe. Brilliant and inviting colors, chiseled and intricate shapes, and aromas that seem to take you to another place are just some of the pleasures that exist here. The textures of the plants and the grass feel so warm and inviting begging you to not just touch, but to embrace. It has the sense of something so familiar and yet I can't remember ever being here before.

It appears much larger than I had originally thought it was. I continue to walk and see a meadow filled with wildflowers up ahead.

I take off running and yelling with abandon through this amazing place that I never would have believed existed. My arms reach out like wings of a bird as my hands brush past the tops of the wildflowers. I am laughing from the depths of my being.

"Ahhh, can you believe this!" I shout, "Ammoris, this is incredible!"

He stood there with satisfaction exuding from his smile.

"I know friend, and it is yours."

"What do you mean?" I say with an inquisitive look.

"Do you remember this place?"

"No, I don't think so."

"Do you remember the first time you sat in the chair?"

"Oh my," I say as the memory comes back. "But, that looked nothing like this. It was full of rocks and nothing was growing like this," I say as I recall the memory. And then, as I replay the image of that memory over what my eyes now see, the reality hits me. "How is that possible?"

"This Alois, is your life's work. It's your garden."

"Yeah, but no one told me that I was doing this. How did I do this?"

"One rock at a time," he says smiling.

"But how did all the plants and trees and flowers get here?"

"It is natural that things will grow when the things that would keep them from growing are removed."

"So, all I had to do was carry the rocks?"

"And receive the seeds that I was planting in your heart."

"Wow, who would've thought that all of my life down there was building something here."

"Haha, unfortunately, not many these days," he says chuckling. "But that's all going to change, right?"

"But how could it change?"

"Because, Alois, they're reading your story right now, and the power of story is in the experience of truth. As they say, 'change a man's mind and he will walk steadily on that path for the rest of his life, but change a man's heart and even the world around him will alter its course."

A final note...

I believe it is impossible to collect all of the thoughts and realities of prayer and connection to God in one place. The experience of God is truly unique to every individual. My hope is that this picture of one man's experience will drive you, not to replicate, but to search out the answer to the question of, 'what is your chair?'

Some may believe that I am attempting to create a theology on origins and earth experiences. If this is your primary thought upon finishing this book, then please understand that this is not my intention. However, you are welcome to read Jeremiah 1:5 and contemplate the benefits of the possibility that we existed before our existence on this earth.

Writings like these are meant to be the stirring in the soul and the distant shout across the valley, declaring: It is time, to set out on the greatest adventure this earth has to offer!

If this work is theologically correct by someone's standard, so be it. But friend, that is not the intent. The intent is that you would find the best friend of your life, and never leave His side.

I do not intend this for the masses, but the few who relish an adventure and call upon danger and risk, as stepping stones to the abundant life.

Are you one of these?

I pray that you are, and that the continued ticking of the clock makes it evident.

When you close this book and put it down, I encourage you to say this simple prayer:

"Please Jesus, help me to be your friend."

-stephen santos

Reflective Questions

What do you think are the most important characteristics of a friendship?

_____

_____

_____

_____

_____

_____

When have you experienced these from God?

_____

_____

_____

_____

_____

_____

Are there any practical steps you can take to further your friendship with God?

_____

_____

_____

_____

_____

_____

What are the things in your life, (objects or relationships) that have a tendency to distract you from the mindset of heaven being your home someday?

_____

_____

_____

_____

_____

_____

List out all the things that you are excited about experiencing in Heaven?

_____

_____

_____

_____

_____

_____

What is the first thing you think you will say to Jesus, when you meet Him in Heaven?

_____

_____

_____

_____

_____

_____

Take some time to pray and ask Jesus to show you where are areas and ways that you could be a better friend to Him. List them out below.

_____

_____

_____

_____

_____

_____

_____

_____

_____

_____

_____

_____

In one year what do you hope will be different in your life, in response to what you've experienced through this story? Write it down, and then ask Jesus to lead you on the path toward that change.

_____
_____
_____
_____
_____
_____
_____
_____
_____
_____
_____

About the Author

Stephen lives in South Carolina with his family. He has done everything from carpentry to writing music. From teaching children who did not have a stable home-life to washing the dishes at his own home. And from leading his kids on adventures in the woods to loving his neighbors, whoever they may be.

He finds great joy in sharing his own story with others; the one where he was led out of religion by Love.

At the end of his life he is looking forward to answering the one question he believes God will ask him.

"How well did you follow my Son?"

And to this end he writes books, he writes songs, he swings a hammer, he serves and loves his family, he encourages those around him and he prays for broken hearts and broken bodies. But more important and precious to him than any of that, he talks with his friend Jesus about all of it. He has become convinced that if he does everything while walking with Jesus, he will truly have the privilege and blessing of The Abundant Life.

More writings

If you enjoyed reading 'Before the Clock Ticks', you will love experiencing 'The Compass Series'. Unlike most series, which are linear on a timeline, the Compass Series actually walks around one storyline for the first 3 books. It is one story from three vantage points. Each book fills in more details about the main characters and is written from a different character's perspective. The final book is what pulls all of the experience together and places it into your own life journey!

You can find out more about Stephen's current books as well as soon to be released books at:
www.stephensantos.com
There, you will also find other childrens books, short stories, writings and songs.

Made in the USA
Middletown, DE
12 May 2025